THE WHITE REVIEW

21

T0155088

THE TRANSVERSE PATH (*or* NATURE'S LITTLE SECRET)   MIKE SLACK

THE ICE PLANT / ISBN 978-0-9992655-0-5

New York
May 3–6, 2018

FRIEZE
ART
FAIR

2P59

A SIGHT OF MANAHATTA IN THE TOWERING NEEDLE
MULTI-FACETED INSIGHT OF THE FLY IN THE STRINGLESS LABYRINTH
– Frank O'Hara

Rhapsody, excerpt from *Lunch Poems* by Frank O'Hara. Used by permission of City Light Books. Photography: Clément Pascal.

Media partner

Global lead partner
Deutsche Bank

Marvin Gaye Chetwynd
Ze & Per

Sadie Coles   HQ

22 February – 07 April 2018
Tuesday–Saturday 11–6

Sadie Coles HQ
62 Kingly Street London W1B 5QN

www.sadiecoles.com

Victoria Miro VENICE

Chantal Joffe

IL CAPRICORNO · SAN MARCO 1994
30124 VENICE · ITALY

14 APRIL – 19 MAY 2018

Published by The White Review, March 2018
Edition of 1,800

Printed by Unicum, Tilburg
Typeset in Nouveau Blanche

ISBN No. 978-0-9957437-3-1

The White Review is a registered charity (number 1148690)

The White Review, 243 Knightsbridge, London SW7 1DN
www.thewhitereview.org

EDITORIAL

During his interview with Claudia Rankine in this issue, Kayo Chingonyi raises the subject of what role the arts might play in a period of 'national emergency'. Discussing artists' responses to recent tragedies, the two poets agree that 'to think of [art] as something that happens in seclusion from lived experience feels wrongheaded in the world we live in'. As we put this issue together, this idea has been greatly on our minds, and it resonates throughout the magazine. In her piece exploring the ethical implications of prisoners' visual representations, Hatty Nestor asks 'how empathy could materialise as visual art'; we hope that the pieces which follow share a spirit of enquiry, compassion and engagement with our complicated times.

The past few months – since our fabled summer party on the rooftop of Bold Tendencies, when hundreds crowded onto hay bales to hear Claire-Louise Bennett's mesmerising reading – have been a period of transition at *The White Review*. This issue appears in a brand new design by Thomas Swann; it is the first under a new editorial team led by Željka Marošević and Francesca Wade. We have launched an anthology, featuring highlights from the magazine's first twenty issues, and a poet's prize (the winning portfolio, by Lucy Mercer, will be published in issue 22). In response to a growing concern at the shrinking number of outlets providing accessible and incisive arts coverage, we've begun publishing regular reviews of new books and exhibitions online, alongside poetry, fiction, interviews and essays. We've hatched plans for events across the UK, established new collaborations, and designed some enviable tote bags, now for sale on our revamped website.

In this issue, the personal and the political collide in bold and unexpected ways. Speaking in advance of her major Tate Modern retrospective, Joan Jonas reflects on a growing sense of environmental consciousness in her performance and installation work. Alev Scott reports from the Balkans on the legacy of the Ottoman Empire, while Megan Hunter explores the connections (physical and psychical) between writing and pregnancy. We are delighted to present fiction and poetry from a range of new and established voices, traversing far-flung realms, from the nocturnal Berlin of Johanna Hedva's 'Jonah' (where the protagonist's attempts to 'recuperate' are thwarted by a forgotten name and a yeast infection), to the newly inhabited island of Sascha Macht's 'The Horror', where the teenage narrator's morbid fascination with horror films mirrors the dystopia emerging in his own life. We're also thrilled to present the first in a new series of roundtable conversations – see p. 26 for more on this new venture for the magazine.

It's an immense privilege to be invited to build on the work of Ben Eastham and Jacques Testard, whose formidable vision, editorial eye and logistical flair have made this magazine a home for the most ambitious and innovative writing over the past seven years. We hope you'll find the same values prevail in the writing and art present here, as we embark on an exciting new era for *The White Review*.

CLAUDIA RANKINE INTERVIEW

Of all the books to enter the wider consciousness in the last decade, *Citizen* is the one to which I have returned most frequently. The book comes up in conversation in an astonishing array of situations, all of which serve to illustrate one thing: there is an appetite at the moment for discourse, for enquiry, for the posing of important and difficult questions. This tendency might not be anything new, but the media through which we can express it have multiplied in the last few years. Instagram and Tumblr poets are now part of popular culture, and the boundaries that divide poetry from other creative modes are being called into question. What does it matter if a text is or isn't a poem as we commonly understand that term; what does that text make us feel? This is the question that sits at the heart of Claudia Rankine's artistic practice, a practice which centres the art itself, the text, asking what form it should take to realise its potential rather than trying to bend that work into an existing shape so that it is recognisable as X or Y. This is a textual account of a conversation I was lucky enough to have with Claudia Rankine while she was in London for Poetry International at the Southbank Centre. Our conversation took place over breakfast – poached eggs on toast, if I recall – in a wonderfully apposite location, the riverside bar of Mondrian London, a hotel that borders on being a gallery space, which sits next to the Sea Containers HQ of Ogilvy and Mather, a short walk from Tate Modern. What follows cannot capture the sound of clinking glasses and laughter that punctuated our conversation, but let that sit in your mind as you read and enter the mind of one of anglophone poetry's most generous and engaged practitioners. KAYO CHINGONYI

TWR I get the impression that race is something that comes up in every interview. Do you feel a pressure to speak about it?

CR No. If I feel a pressure it's from society, what's happening in the world. I don't feel the pressure is coming from interviewers, the pressure is coming from the kind of injustice that is so palpable that it's amplified in my life and the lives of Americans and the lives of Europeans; the turn towards a more fascist orientation. I think I've always been the kind of writer who responds to what's in my life. You go to bed and you wake up and you find out that undocumented students who could be in your classroom are getting deported. I'm more surprised that people shut that stuff down.

TWR There's an interesting moment within *Citizen* where the setting is London and there's this feeling that race is not something that can be broached, or it isn't the role of certain people to talk about race. The provocation I get from your work is that it is up to all of us to talk about it.

CR I don't like telling people what they have to do. I think people should do what they want to do, especially in the realm of creative work. I think you can't really legislate the imagination, and if you do it's something else: it's journalism, it's sociology. For me as somebody who is a creative artist, either writing or visually, it is part of my imagination, and it would sadden me to think that somebody who is a creative would shut an impulse down if it presents itself for fear of dating the work or of upsetting somebody, if it is in fact an integral part of the things that they're thinking about. I'm not advocating for anybody stepping into an arena that they're not in, because what is that?

TWR I do find your work inspiring at that level. I think the work you're doing, in *Citizen* and now with The Racial Imaginary Institute, is emboldening for my generation of writers and a number of other generations and audiences. I'm particularly inspired by that, not just in relation to race but also in relation to the form and matter of poetry; what constitutes a poem on the page and what constitutes an interdisciplinary work. So, when I think about *Don't Let Me Be Lonely*, which looks at how our lives are increasingly mediated through a number of different spheres and media, the fact that our poetic culture didn't previously reflect that is so strange. When I started to interact with your work it made so much sense for it to be presented that way:

accepting that as poetry didn't feel problematic.

CR I'm not the first poet who has worked in the prose-poem form – the French were doing it a long time ago. I think people get into these boxes in terms of what the form should be, and I really believe that form and content should always be in dialogue. When I work on something I think, 'What are the tools I need to make this be the best it can be?' and if it were a song lyric then I would do it. That's a stretch, but if I knew how or I could collaborate with people; if it were a sonnet then I would write a book of sonnets. It's not that I have anything against traditional form, it's just that in thinking about race you're thinking about people's lives. A book like *Citizen* was dependent on stories of people, and so one wanted to find a form that could hold that. In *Don't Let Me Be Lonely* I felt like the sentence helped me more than the line, so I went to the sentence. These are questions one has every time you walk into the making of a poem.

TWR Was that understanding of poetry present early in your writing life? What constitutes your early writing life? Were you writing from the time you were a child or in your teens?

CR No, I started writing in college. I was really influenced by the work of Adrienne Rich, James Baldwin, Samuel Beckett, W.B. Yeats, and I'm a big reader of fiction, I love J.M. Coetzee. It took time for me to understand that everything I learned from all those people could help me in my work. Initially I was working more in form, I was producing what I was being fed, but the older I got the more I was reading. I was reading people like Charles Bernstein, Lyn Hejinian, [Eugenio] Montale, and so then your ideas about what can happen inside the poem become activated and you start to experiment.

TWR To my mind the experimentation in your work is very integrated, and so it makes a lot of sense that you would mention Yeats on the one hand and Lyn Hejinian on the other. It seems clear in your work that disparate influences have been brought together over a long period of time...

CR ...and [Edward Kamau] Brathwaite, what he does on the page is incredible and how he takes over that space as a kind of canvas. He's someone that also I look to. And then Derek Walcott and his use of sound... All of them are out there and they can help you, but you don't have to replicate what they do.

TWR   Can you think of a moment that you felt, in relation to your own work, 'This piece is doing the work I want to do'?

CR   Well, my publisher, when I wrote *Don't Let Me Be Lonely*, got rid of me. When they got the manuscript they said, 'This is not poetry'. It was one of those moments where I thought, 'I'm disappointed about this but this is what I need, I'm not gonna change anything to conform to somebody's idea about what the market needs, and if the consequence is I find myself without a publisher, I find myself without a publisher.' It didn't take long to get another one. These decisions are not without consequences, but if they're truly yours then you stand behind them and you take what you get in terms of people's responses. But it doesn't bother me so much because I know it's what I want to do. Which is not to say I couldn't be wrong; I could be wrong, but let me be wrong on my terms, and what am I wrong about? Wrong that I want to express myself in this way? In my case I feel very lucky that I was able to find my audience. Somebody like John Ashbery, people didn't like his work at all in the beginning, and they said it didn't make any sense. You can go back and read all the reviews, and he began to teach people how to read him and now nobody thinks there's anything odd about John Ashbery's writing.

TWR   I think that's an important part of the process of finding something distinctive. I think if there is nothing particularly distinctive about one's work and lots of people like it immediately, the scary thing is that one can get comfortable and get trapped in a pattern of churning out more of the same every two or three years.

CR   One of the things I love about Anne Carson's work is the way in which the form and content meet and how exciting it is that each book does its own thing. Which is not to say I love everything she does, but I anticipate everything she does because I know that she's thinking, 'How does this thing best show itself, best speak itself?' Jorie Graham has a new book out right now that also does incredible things around how information, how memory, comes to us. With Graham I love what she does in terms of sound and language – coming up with new sounds to talk about that space in terms of the articulation of memory. I agree with you, I think the poets that I love create form for content.

TWR   What's your perspective on where you publish?

CR   It doesn't really matter to me where I publish. I rarely publish poetry; usually I publish right before a book comes out unless I'm responding, like I've written a poem in response to something and then I will send it to an editor and say 'consider this'. That's reflective of the point I am in my career right now. Earlier on I, like everyone, wanted to be published in *The New Yorker* or *The Paris Review* or *The Southern Review*. By the time I was in my forties it seemed like there were so many reviews that everybody was reading and all my friends were publishing reviews that it became less and less important where you published, you were really happy to give your work to people who were like-minded.

TWR   There seems to be a healthier journal culture in the States. It feels as if, at every level of poetry publishing, beautiful things can be produced and it doesn't matter as much if your poems are in a big journal because even the smaller ones have a dedicated following.

CR   I think also because we have this MFA culture in the States where a lot of young people are studying writing. You have this internal market that's not determined by public consumption, it's automatic with those students, and many of them are the ones who start these journals and so we have a different reading public. I don't know if here you have the same MFA culture?

TWR   It's beginning to be that way. The Creative Writing MA programme has become part of what most universities offer if they specialise in the humanities, and at most universities there has to be some form of creative writing course at the undergraduate, if not the postgraduate, level. It's a growth area.

CR   I think people have recognised that it actually is good to sponsor creative expression. Writing especially is a good skill to have, and not every one of those students will continue to do it for the rest of their lives but it's still a good skill to have, like learning how to swim. To understand what language can do, to become a closer reader, a better reader, and to improve your writing skills as a point of communication.

TWR   I was wondering also about your interaction with, and continual return to, visual stimuli, not only as an influence on written expression but also the incorporation of works of visual art into your work when written expression is insufficient.

There are prints of art works, video installations of your poems... Are you always working in this cross-disciplinary manner?

CR   I am, because I think if there is one thing my work does, one thing it's invested in, it's seeing. What does it mean to see this thing happen? I'm really interested in affect. I read a lot of critical work by affect theorists. One wants the language to embody what is seen and what is felt and what is heard. It helps to then be able to visualise the unnamable. If I have to take the image myself, I'll take it, but there are so many visual artists out there that I'm willing to buy the rights to replicate what they do better. When you're in this realm of talking about relationships between people of different races, so much of it is triggered by what is seen. You could be on the phone and suddenly you walk into the room and you're a black man and, according to the white imagination, you're someone to be targeted, not someone to be welcomed. The space suddenly has no space for you. And all of that has to be negotiated by that person and by you, so it's something to see.

TWR   Talking of seeing, I was really moved by a set of critical responses you made to Tony Hoagland's poem 'The Change', which discussed the racialised seeing in 'The Change' and poems like it, poems which Major Jackson has called poems of 'racial encounter', where blackness exists as some otherness which is equated always with the bodily, the bestial, poems in which blackness cannot occupy the space of kinship and friendship, or welcome, as you just put it. I was moved by the inclusion of Toyin Ojih Odutola's work in *Citizen* because of the ways in which blackness is, in Odutola's work, this radiant, resplendent, glorious thing. So, though her subjects are not necessarily always black, depicting them as having black skin expands our sense of what blackness can include and what blackness is in terms of its associations.

CR   First of all I agree with you. Toyin's work is incredible and the pieces themselves are amazing, and so is her discipline and poetics around what she's going for in the use of black ink or charcoal or blackness as a material to work with in these portraits is. She has an opening at the Whitney and a new book coming out called *The Treatment* which has all the portraits in the series called 'The Treatment' of white drawn with black ballpoint.

TWR   What was your first encounter with Odutola's work?

CR   I came across her work initially in *Art In America* or something like that, and I was just blown away by the beauty of the portraits. I don't know if Toyin intended this, but that sense of 'You think I'm black? I'll show you blackness', the texture of the skin that she draws is illuminated... It's almost like it's winking at you off the page. There's no attempt to be representational even though you see these people as people. I found that electrifying and that led me to read everything that she's written, and my first encounter with the work was to go to a show at Jack Shainman Gallery, which is where I met her. I find that visual artists are creating a discourse of thinking about blackness and historicising or reframing and creating counter-narratives around portrayals of blackness that are incredibly exciting to me. It gives me both pleasure and information as I go back to my own work and think about how to bring presence into the actual language. One of the things I really want to work on is asking how language activates black joy. It's something that Fred Moten talks a lot about. I feel somewhere down the line that's my next challenge as a writer. One sees that in music, like jazz, which brings forward what is painful in the history but also what is joyful. That's why we miss Prince so much and what we love about Solange and her new album and *Lemonade* and Rihanna... my God, Rihanna!

TWR   There is an unapologetic exuberance and flamboyance to all those projects...
CR   ... and Kanye, as crazy as he is.

TWR   There's something about that attitude which comes from blackness, because blackness is something you cannot step outside of once you find yourself to exist within it. There's a degree to which you can accept a black subjectivity or distance yourself from it, but, as you said, if I walk into a space like this, I'm seen as a black man; I'm forced to engage with it. So if we engage with it exuberantly, there is a resistance in that, even if that engage-ment is merely frivolous (men draped in Versace, Lamborghinis, and all these tropes of luxury). Even at their most problematic there is resistance embedded in those acts.
CR   I think when we're in a world where black people are not considered human, any engagement and assertion of one's life is resistance. To live is resistance, to thrive is resistance, to have a sustained

daily-ness is resistance. At the end of the day, if we were gone it wouldn't matter to a lot of people.

TWR   Since you mention Fred Moten, I wonder how you respond to his formulation of Black Social Life: the space of resistance that comes out of the creation of counter-structures of knowledge-sharing and social interaction within blackness. I'm thinking especially about something Fred Moten said, in response to Steve McQueen's *12 Years a Slave*, at a talk I went to: 'Shame is the modality in which blackness is lived'. If that is true, something as simple as a social space which is joyful can be a space of healing. How do you feel about that in relation to being here, in the bar of the Mondrian; how do you feel about gaining access to things through your work and your mind that some people in the world did not expect you to have access to?
CR   First of all I don't think I'm given access to this space. This space is as much mine as anyone else's. If you can pay the bill it is your space. The sense of white ownership of these spaces is part of the problem. The spaces in and of themselves are neutral. What creates the illusion that they're owned by whiteness is what the bodies who inhabit them do. So if you populate the spaces with white people and the habits of those people are to behave as if they own that space, that's where the perception comes from. I feel as if I have access to any space, and I know that much has been done to keep me out of these spaces, it's not without its history; I understand how much work has been done to get me into these spaces, but it still always was my space. It's a space and just because people behave in one way or another, it doesn't change the possibility of the space, or else I wouldn't be in this space now.

TWR   Who do you feel, in poetry, has been working to reframe our discourse around ownership of and entitlement to space?
CR   People like Amiri Baraka – 'S.O.S – Calling All Black People' – he's done such important work. Not all of it as generous as it could be, but still important. Audre Lorde has done incredible work, Adrienne Rich. I could go on. There have been so many writers who have engaged in freeing up our imagination in terms of even what you can say. Sonia Sanchez is amazing, Tracie Morris, Jericho Brown – I don't know if you know his work. Robin Coste Lewis has a new book out that has done really important work in terms of creating counter-narratives around the portrayals of blackness in

visual arts. People are doing all kinds of things that are really exciting to me. Kevin Young has a new book out. I'm going to be here in the month of June and I just want to read a lot of British poets because the one failing in my life is that you get immersed in one culture. The events tend to circle around American poetry. You're not opening *The New Yorker* and reading international poets as much as one would like, which is not true in fiction, I think because poetry is such a small market in the US anyway that the space they give is just to a few people so they don't come from the outside too much.

TWR   So you think of it as a small world, the literary landscape?
CR   Yeah, the controlled literary landscape, the one that you get without too much work: *The New Yorker, The Paris Review...* those kinds of journals are propped up by the establishment and therefore made available to everyone without that person having to do anything special.

TWR   I think in the UK there is a good deal of work responding to trends in American poetry but there is also a lot that is not available to American poetry audiences.
CR   Like what?

TWR   I think within the States there is less of a sense of cross-section because the poetry scene is bigger than it is here. Here we get a lot of surveys of what is going on in different parts of the US – Buffalo, or Iowa, or Vermont. But in the States, from inside it, I imagine it is harder to get that kind of wider perspective.
CR   For me, I feel like much of my time is spent not with what's happening in Buffalo but what's happening in Ferguson, what's happening in DC, what's happening in terms of justice issues inside our country. I think there are poets who are more cognisant of the goings on in poetry circles. Right now there is a conference in Arizona, but if I'm choosing between a conference in Arizona and a conference on black pessimism or a talk by Bryan Stevenson on what's happening in mass incarceration, that's where I'm going.

TWR   I think what poets here are responding to is both the situation of national emergency in the States and the response to that from poets, whereas when you're inside it I imagine the response from poets, whether you are a poet or not, is not the most important thing.

CR   It's not the most immediate thing; the immediate thing is the thing. That's the thing that you're responding to and the thing you're talking to people about. I'm not talking to people about poetry, I'm talking to people about what happened to Michael Brown or what the legislation around DACA (Deferred Action for Childhood Arrivals) is, the march for black women in Washington. Those are things that we're talking about, at least I'm talking about, and not necessarily with poets or not only with poets.

TWR   Maybe those are the more pressing discussions in relation to the making of creative work. To think of it as something that happens in seclusion from lived experience feels wrongheaded in the world we live in.

CR   I'm really interested in what y'all have written about Grenfell. Were people interviewed, what did people have to say, how is that showing up in the writing? What is the response? Because that is a national tragedy, especially given that many of those people were undocumented, especially given that the word 'immigrant' is a mask for racial exclusion. What's going on, are there memorials around the tower? I can't believe that I haven't seen that stuff. That's what I'm interested in.

TWR   I think in the immediate aftermath there was an attempt from the poetry community to respond not just at the level of 'let's do an event' or 'let's do some poems', but also at the level of physical presence. Lots of poets have been lobbying and organising. Grenfell stands as a monument, the thing stands there, and if you live in this city there is no missing it. There is one poet I know of, Jay Bernard, who is engaging concurrently at the level of activism and at the level of creative work by drawing parallels between the New Cross fire and Grenfell. There's never been any answers about New Cross, and the way that dovetails with what has happened in relation to Grenfell creates this new context.

CR   That's the amplification of institutional neglect. It's the same white supremacy, the same centralising of whiteness that says that other people don't need our attention even though poor whites were in that tower.

TWR   In relation to this question of centralising whiteness as the normative position from which other subjectivities deviate, what's the direction you want to go in with The Racial Imaginary Institute?

CR   The idea of The Racial Imaginary Institute is to curate events that create counter-narratives for whiteness and for blackness and people of colour, because we have been told stories that exclude histories that are part of the reality of those stories. The thing that has been normalised and the activity that has been erased has to do with whiteness. A little work in bringing forward that history, that orientation, that information is necessary, missing, and useful at this point. I think the work that David Olusoga is doing in Bristol is exactly what we want The Racial Imaginary Institute to do. It's the bringing forward of that which has been suppressed. He talks about merchants being renamed as slave owners, and that seems like a little thing but it's important for understanding how manufactured cotton came from the slave plantations. Reorienting the stories so that we understand the connections that persisted despite the narrative that Britain was the first country to get out of the slave trade; that's not even true, the Danes were. We're really interested in work that looks at all of that stuff which hasn't been said. If you go to the website you'll see work by Toyin, you'll see essays by Lauren Berlant reframing the election of Trump, you'll see white women talking to their children about what it means to live in a country where white supremacy is a part of the orientation of their lives, you'll see Nona Faustine's photography where you can't get to the memorials without walking through a cloud of blackness. How do you get imperialism and the history of colonialism not to detach themselves in present-day representation? The artists and writers on the website so far are a few of the people who are doing that, and we are looking for work by everybody and anybody. People send work to us and we are more than enthusiastic about including it on the site. The reason why we started as a website was because we wanted to use the most democratised engine so that it's constantly mobile. In the design of the site we made sure that it didn't matter what the format was, so it can hold video, it can hold print, it can hold visual, it can hold audio, we can have papers, we can have poems and we can have short stories. We're looking to do a blog, we just need somebody to do it. One of the things I would really love the site to do that it's not doing now is respond to events in time. If we had a podcast, for example, two people could talk about a new movie that opened. Whatever discussions are alive and present, we would like to weigh in on them.

TWR   It's a very important venture, not least because it re-centres the question about who should be... not should, but how we engage in this discourse in a manner that is transformative rather than merely retaliationary. I think the online 'call-out' culture of owning and expressing anger is a part of the process, but healing doesn't come from that necessarily, it comes from a project like The Racial Imaginary Institute.

CR   I don't even know if it's healing, I think reality comes from a project like that. If some guy was a slave owner, I'm not saying you need to pull down his statue, I'm just saying that on that plaque, if you look down, it should say slave owner so that we see the full picture and the truth of what is before us. That's all I'm asking. I don't care, pull it down, keep it up, but if you're gonna put it in front of me, tell me what really happened.

TWR   I think that's crucial at this point, it really is.

CR   Yeah, because a lot of white people don't know either, so they believe the rhetoric around the goodness of whiteness. I think people don't realise what they were born into and therefore what they bring forward.

TWR   What's damaging, also, is if you exist within a structure that inflates your sense of self-worth then the inverse of that is that if you find yourself to be ordinary but the world at large tells you you're exceptional, how do you square that away? I've noticed this in relation to the work of poets who believe that their white subjectivity feels, to them, inauthentic or not sufficiently interesting so they embark on a process of self-effacement in their work in an attempt to be on 'the right side of history'. What a project like yours is doing is taking away this notion of a wrong or right side of history and focusing instead on presenting history in its fullness.

CR   White people are like, 'I don't feel comfortable.' Comfortable what? Telling the history? Speaking from where I actually exist? We just have to start doing that.

TWR   Do you feel that you are now able to do the work that you want to do as a poet?

CR   The process of getting to this moment where I feel clear about what I'm doing, I'm very happy to be here. I feel a kind of mobility within my own creative energies that other times have felt more of a struggle, but I also think I could lose it any moment depending on where the next thing goes. There's always a way in which you start a project and you really feel that you're at the beginning again. I'm really appreciative of the cumulative flexibility and mobility of the synapse connecting the research, the teaching, the writing and the playwriting that I'm in right this minute, but when these projects I'm involved in come to a close I don't necessarily know if that will stay with me and if there is another building that will have to happen for the next iteration.

TWR   I'm very excited to have that work in the world in whatever form it takes. Do you feel playwriting is something you'll continue? Is that part of the new work you're envisioning, or the space you want to enter next, or do you begin simply by asking what the work demands?

CR   Usually it's what the work demands. The play that I'm working on at the moment that opens in February, *The White Card*, I wanted to do it because I really wanted to have a public conversation. I was really shocked at people's inability to speak in a sustained way about race. White people became defensive, black people shut down, people of colour were unclear as to how these discussions related to them, and so I thought it would be good to work in a form that allowed me to force the conversation to continue, and the only form that presented itself for that was theatre and playwriting. That's why *The White Card* had to be a play, it wouldn't have worked as an essay or anything that was a private moment between me and the page. Once that is up and running I'm at the beginning of the third book in the American Lyric series, and right now it's a book on whiteness. And when that is complete I don't know what's next.

K. C.,
October 2017

FACING FUTURE FEELINGS: THE PORTRAIT OF CHELSEA MANNING

HATTY NESTOR

Last autumn I listened to an episode from the 1999 'Lock Up' series of *This American Life*, which explored the way prisoners represent their identities visually once they have been released. During the podcast, an ex-detainee explained that during incarceration he and his fellow convicts 'had very little to see or look at, in terms of variety, in terms of what one had become used to. Seeing people come and go, different distances, different colours, different lives, all just one vague big grey soup.' What struck me most about his comments was how starkly prison-industrial complexes violate the agency of those they detain, limiting prisoners' ability to connect with each other and the outside world, and most of all, denying any assertion of individual identity. I began to wonder how writing and visual art could help represent prisoners deemed invisible by wider society. Interviews, such as the one in the podcast, contribute to building a biographical narrative of a subject – but what about photographs, portraits and paintings? What might an ethical portrait of a prisoner look like? Could art be used as a tool to give agency back to those on the inside? Or rather, who do prisoners rely on to construct images of them from the outside, in the face of a system which seeks to siphon off all humanity?

*

The dehumanisation of transgender prisoners is by no means unfamiliar, but the trial, prosecution and release of Chelsea Manning has shifted the rhetoric of both media and personal representation into a different realm. During her incarceration I knew of Manning as someone both famous and infamous, whose identity as a trans woman and committer of treason has been widely sensationalised. A United States Army soldier, Manning was convicted under the Espionage Act and for a number of other offences in 2013 after she 'leaked' over 700,000 sensitive diplomatic documents to the secret sharing site Wikileaks. The files contained war logs from Afghanistan and Iraq, diplomatic cables from the state department and documents on Guantanamo Bay. After pleading guilty to ten of the twenty-two charges of which she was accused, Manning was sentenced to thirty-five years imprisonment at Fort Leavenworth, Kansas. Several years before her sentencing, she had also spent three years in detention centres such as Camp Arifjan in Kuwait, alongside prisons in Virginia, Kansas and Maryland, where she waited to hear the length of her sentence. There, Manning was held for twenty-three hours a day in solitary confinement, with no sunlight.

As Manning's case unfolded, I kept many jottings, notes and screenshots of news reports. What grips me about her case is the complexity of its legality in relation to war and surveillance, intensified by the complex ethical questions produced by her gender transition. Who was this woman, who appeared to be so integral to, yet so mistreated by, the state? In the margins of a printed-out *TIME* article from 2015 entitled 'Chelsea Manning Can No Longer Be Called "He" by the Military, Court Rules', I wrote: 'How does the prison-industrial complex monitor, represent and treat transgender inmates?' A simple question, but I soon discovered that the attention given to Manning's case was symptomatic of the widespread brutality of the American justice system. Transgender inmates can arouse confusion and rage in society at large, making them more vulnerable to mistreatment and violence. They are sanctioned, ignored and deemed unworthy of protection. Throughout my research I found that it is usual for transgender inmates to be admitted to the incorrectly gendered prison. Activist group Black & Pink's 2015 national LGBTQ prisoner survey 'Coming Out of Concrete Closets' reported that '23 per cent of transgender, nonbinary gender, and Two-Spirit respondents are currently taking hormones in prison, while an overwhelming 44 per cent report being denied access to hormones they requested.' Manning was refused hormone treatment, rejected for psychological help and relentlessly placed in solitary confinement as a penal strategy. Her detention – her isolation and torture – is the story of many; it is by no means exceptional.

It fascinated me to consider how empathy could materialise as visual art. I wanted to meet Manning, I wanted to talk to her personally and understand her own desire for representation. In retrospect, collecting these articles was a way for me to reappropriate news reports – to uncover alternative narratives surrounding Manning's case, avenues through which to interpret her mistreatment. The headlines were painful reminders of Manning's suffering. I began to wonder what would have happened if Manning's sentence hadn't been commuted by Barack Obama in 2017: how much longer would she have been kept in solitary confinement?

Detention is imposed in order to sanction, isolate and divide. The rise in supermax prisons (originating in Arizona and California) since the 1980s has amplified the prosecution and punishment of those deemed delinquent by society. A particularly harrowing example is the recently closed 'tent city' in Arizona, a fully functioning concentration camp in Maricopa County, advertised to those it incarcerates as an alternative to serving longer sentences. Inmates are told that if they submit themselves to living in temperatures as high as 120 Fahrenheit they can have days shaved off their sentence, as a capacity-enhancing possibility for 'doing time'. It is very difficult to gain access to these prisons, and consequently I have never visited one, though I have exchanged letters via Jmail (an online service for writing electronic messages to prisoners) with a woman who was incarcerated in Pelican Bay State Prison, Del Norte County, California. She explained that in supermax prisons, psychological damage is perpetually exacerbated by government authorities. Due to the privatisation of prisons across the United States, those detained are seen as capital, little more than objects for financial gain.

Prisons are a tool of power and rule, and manifest as a form of domination and oppression. But a representation of an individual prisoner has the power to restore and extend the visibility of all inmates and their legitimacy to wider society. In her essay 'On the Intersection of the Military and the Prison Industrial Complex', Manning wrote that 'the prison industrial complex had the power to imprison me and label me as an offender for life'. Within prison, communication technologies such as mobile phones and the internet are limited; prisoners communicate with the outside via paid outlets Jmail, Corrlinks and JPay, as well as hand-written letters and phone calls, which often only last fifteen minutes and are regulated by prison authorities – all part of the way prisoners become invisible to the outside. While incarcerated, Manning regularly wrote articles for *The Guardian*, and it was a point of public discussion as to whether this counted as an unfair liberty, manipulating her profile within society. But in July 2016, the news that Manning faced solitary confinement – and the ceasing of her usual scheduled phone calls – for her suicide attempt at Fort Leavenworth horrified activists. There is an aggressive undervaluation of mental health in institutionalised settings such as prison – supposedly a site of 'reform' – where inmates are often denied therapies, hormone treatment and counselling. Social deprivation, in an interpersonal sense, is not just constructed by limited human contact, but also by the constraints imposed by the physicality of inhumane environments. In an article for *The Guardian* in May 2016, Manning described that whilst placed in solitary confinement – in a 6 × 8 ft cell – 'I was not allowed to lie down. I was not allowed to lean my back against the cell wall. I was not allowed to exercise.' Such an environment only furthers isolation and deepens identity issues, making any affirming connection with the outside world all the more urgent and valuable.

*

A month before her arrest in April 2010, Manning attached a black-and-white photograph in an email to retired Sergeant 1st Class Paul Adkins with the subject line 'My Problem'. This photograph of Manning in a car seat wearing a blonde wig and make-up – since widely circulated – has been considered her first attempt at asserting her gender identity. The email reportedly contained the line: 'I don't know what to do anymore, and the only "help" that seems to be available is severe punishment and/or getting rid of me.' When she was trapped in solitary confinement, the Chelsea Manning Support Network released a similar statement on Manning's behalf: 'I need help. I am not getting any. I have asked for help time and time again for six years and through five separate confinement locations.' After the release of such viscerally charged statements, and after a week-long period of hunger strike, Manning was permitted sex reassignment surgery in September 2016.

Two years previously, the Chelsea Manning Support Network had decided to commission a portrait of Manning, in an attempt to ensure that her representation in the media would reflect her expression, and mitigate the disjunct in identity she had previously experienced. Under US Army Regulation 190–47, prisoners 'will not be photographed, except in support of medical documentation and for facial identification purposes'. As Manning could not sit for a portrait in prison, there needed to be alternative artistic avenues to mitigate what the Support Network saw as the visual mistreatment of her in the media, to allow Manning to take control of her image from inside Fort Leavenworth. The Support Network approached Alicia Neal, an artist and illustrator from Philadelphia, to create an image that could be utilised across media outlets as Manning's 'official' portrait: an artistic intervention to revolutionise Manning's media coverage. I found Neal's website; her practice appeared kitsch and enigmatic in colour, often finding its subject matter in folklore and paganism. I was curious to know why the Support Network had chosen to contact her specifically. I'd read that she had had to work from photographs of Manning, sending drawings to Fort Leavenworth, waiting for a response and redrawing accordingly. I came to understand that the ethical implications of this image involve every aspect of its conception – from the intention behind the commissioning process, the overcoming of the constraints of prison, through to the creation of the image and its distribution.

Neal's portrait could only be ethical if its pursuit was a realistic representation of Manning. But how was this possible, when she was unable to see Manning in the flesh? The idea of a caricature or impressionist portrait seemed to defeat the purpose of reinstating agency for someone who had so emphatically been denied it. Neal's portrait is a gesture that seeks to preserve and reimagine Manning as human, and not a subject defined by rule and law. This portrait is not just the face of a woman who *needed* an alternative portrait, it is the portrait of a society which misrepresents, and refuses to acknowledge, individuals who do not conform to its expectations.

I knew I could only confront the intricacies of the portrait by speaking directly to Alicia Neal. I wanted to hear how Manning came to trust her; about the dynamics of their intangible relationship. I wanted to know under what conditions the portrait emerged, and who it challenged. Neal promptly replied to my first email, in December 2016, proposing an interview: 'I am happy to help. I'd like to mention first and foremost that I've never had direct contact with Chelsea.' We arranged to talk a week later.

*

Before investigating the image of Manning, it is important to mention that there are many other examples of what I have come to perceive as ethical and unethical portraits of prisoners in society and the media. Courtroom artists undergo the difficult task of representing those on trial objectively, whilst retaining a level of professionalism in a heightened emotional environment. Artists and activists have also explored the role of portraiture as a satirical measure, employing humour as a political act against dehumanisation. A project launched by activist/artists Jeff Greenspan and Andrew Tider in 2015 entitled *Captured: People in Prison Drawing People Who Should Be* sought to draw a comparison between those who are incarcerated for crimes, and those who are not held accountable and walk free – exploring the attendant questions of class and race. I was especially moved by *Prison Landscapes* (2013) by artist Alyse Emdur – a book which brings together a collection of 100 photographs of prisoners as they stand in front of painted backdrops in prison visiting rooms. Many of these reference natural landscapes: waterfalls, tropical beaches and sunsets mount the prisons' grey walls. Also of note is the job of forensic sketch artists, who use image modification/identification, composite imagery, e-fits and postmortem drawings as methods to apprehend or identify those who cannot be found physically. Often the artist interviews the witness or victim in person to gain a first-hand account of their lived experience, which is then translated into visual material for the police. It is these complicated negotiations of constraint, subversion and representation which are so compelling to me, particularly in the case of Manning. I have come to understand an 'ethical portrait' to be a depiction of someone which holds political weight, is integral and empathetic; which challenges marginalisation through a visual image.

Mugshots are a protocol of the justice system's implementation of discipline – they are the least merciful representations of prisoners, which demand their subjects to act as if they are already corpses, staring into the camera with morose expressions, wearing the uniform orange jumpsuits which signal their new societal status. Although Neal's portrait does not intend to mimic a mugshot, it does focus on Manning's face and shoulders, displaying some similarities to traditional portraiture and police photographs. Neal explained that Manning's mugshot, if one existed, was never used in the media, which instead tended to illustrate articles with 'her official military portrait of Bradley'; but, she says, 'I think that it switched into that terrible selfie once she declared that she was transitioning, because there was no other option.' That 'no other option' is imperative here. Neal was keen to explain that the black-and-white selfie of Manning was 'circulated like a mug shot', which was 'very damaging to her image', but it was not Manning herself but the Support Network which decided to commission the new portrait. In replacing the military photograph with all its associations, Neal's portrait serves as a site of solidarity for Manning.

In the portrait Manning is presented as calm, composed and comfortable in her expression and gender, with what Neal has described as a slight 'Mona Lisa smile'. The background is neutral, as is her shirt; the portrait's fundamental purpose of expressing a *lived* experience, as opposed to a speculative artist's impression, shines through. It became increasingly apparent that Neal's ethical position was to put Manning's desired representation first, ahead of her own creative agency as an artist. Neal told me that this portrait – constructed entirely from existing drawings of Manning – differed from her usual mode of working, which would involve extensive photography and discussion with the subject. 'I wanted the portrait to be the best representation of her,' said Neal. 'My main focus was giving her the dignity of at least being seen as who she wants to be... what I thought she would look like realistically, and not like this fantasy character.' The portrait mediates between society's perception of Manning's identity, and the way she truly wants to be seen: it endeavours to uphold her lived reality of the inside from the outside. It demonstrates how our sense of self often forms in union with the conditions of our environment, our experiences and influences – which, in Manning's case, involve subordination. 'I'm not a very political person,' said Neal, 'but I support Chelsea as a trans person, so I feel like this is sort of my contribution.'

Neal told me that many people have speculated whether Manning received 'special treatment' as a political prisoner, being allowed to write, undergo gender transition surgery and have a portrait made. But in 2016, when I interviewed Neal, Manning was still detained in Fort Leavenworth with no future discussion of release, and subject to another twenty-eight years of imprisonment. Release was a hypothetical future imagined by the Chelsea Manning Support Network: until that point Manning remained removed from society, defined and represented by the institutions in which she was incarcerated. Manning wrote about this state of non-being in December 2015 (her sixth Christmas in prison) in an article for *The Guardian*, for which she regularly wrote from within Fort Leavenworth. 'Living in a society that says "Pics or it didn't happen", I wonder if I happened. I sometimes feel less than empty; I feel non-existent.' From this comment, I came to interpret the portrait as a gesture of empathy transformed into an event of justice, a visual representation of existential worth. Manning, Neal suggests, has 'been demonised left and right, and I think it's hard for people to see her as a person... the intention was to make it as serious and conservative as possible so that she would be taken seriously. I wanted to give her the dignity of at least being seen as who she wants to be, because I have trans friends and I've seen them go through the transition and how hard it can be to represent yourself and make people see you as you.' Her work reimagines Manning sympathetically as a political prisoner, and liberates her image from a punitive construct. When the portrait was released on the Chelsea Manning Support Network site in May 2014, there was a sudden shift in the press, as the new image replaced the military photograph; Manning's suffering in relation to her gender identity was no longer hypothetical, but newly validated. Neal's portrait makes the statement that Manning's identity has nothing to do with her imprisonment. It reminds us that we are not solely defined by the institutions and environments we are subject to and conditioned by, that we do not have to stand for the myriad ways in which society is numb to those who are marginalised. My conversations with Neal showed me that images – in contradictory and mysterious ways – can be actions and social commentaries. Her portrait attempts – through medium, form, context and content – to fundamentally change the meaning of what art can *do* in society.

*

A great relief swept over me when Obama granted Manning's clemency on 17 January 2017. Manning was no longer a detainee waiting indefinitely for an end, but a political prisoner who has been redefined as human. Before Manning's release, a Google search for images of her showed three Mannings: the army photograph from before her transition; the grainy, bewigged, monochrome selfie; and Neal's portrait. After her release was announced for 17 May 2017, Manning began to release a steady stream of new public images. First, an Instagram shot of her two feet with the tag line 'First steps of freedom!! :D', followed, a few hours later, by a slice of pizza. Her Instagram – xychelsea87 – operates as a space for humour and self-expression. On Twitter, Manning's use of emoji has become an idiosyncratic appraisal of Trump's presidency. A recurring tweet reading 'We have more power than they do' and '#WeGotThis' is perhaps the most optimistic example of the way Manning is now using her persona as a political self-portrait, employing social media as a tool to reclaim the voice she was denied within prison. 'I could not go on living in the wrong body,' she explained in her first video interview with *ABC News* in May 2017. 'I used to get these feelings where I just wanted to rip my body apart.' Despite these horrifying, visceral words, I felt warmed by seeing her speak on national news, embodying the freedom Neal's portrait sought to create. Among my favourite of her self-portraits is a photograph of her in Times Square smiling enigmatically, with the ABC interview on a large screen behind her.

The magnificent photograph of Manning published three days after her release, where she peers into the camera sideways, dressed in a black, slightly unzipped jacket, is perhaps the most stoic of her current public portraits. It is not a substitute for her experience – it *is* her lived experience. Through choosing how to be photographed, Manning is permitted complete control over her expression, clothing, environment and posture. I read this image as a political action against dehumanisation: a small reminder of the power of empathy.

THE ARK
ANTHONY JOSEPH

From *The Frequency of Magic*.

For Stephen Samuel Gordon: Spaceape.

Sun Ra was on the ark. Prince Nico Mbarga, he was on the ark. So was Art
Taylor and Sonny Simmons, and Bessie Smith and Superblue, all on the ark
and Joe Tex and Mitty Collier, Leon Thomas and the Roaring Lion, even
Robert Aaron and Lou Ciccotelli were abdominally on the ark. The Original
Defosto himself was also on the ark, beat rivers of song upon the omele drum,
just a cutlass carpenter, no skill with timber, four eyed fish were on the ark.
Who playing war and fraid blood? Who playing mas and fraid powder? Who
prevaricate and ruse, throwing holi powder as ritual upon the ark, but don't
want ink or powder to touch their clothes? Who else was on the ark? Max
Roach was on the ark, and Ras Shorty I and David Rudder, Belafonte and
Dolphy, them was high up upon the boat. Babatunde! was on the ark, Olatunji!
mama drum, say you coming to come and you never reach, as far as the leader
house, his records and sawed off speaker box, to boom dub roots all around
the village – bachelor life – and then you hear he bulling some woman in the
congregation, and the shepherd sanding crook-sticks and tapping his foot
when the hymn swing, but is suffer he suffering in silence, because while he
in church, his woman horning him with the leader, and he don't need to be
a see-er man to see, make him burn his own house down, his hand was good,
he was on the ark. Bheti was on the ark, and Vino in pyjamas, the wild moon,
fever in his throat. Performance poet and Stand Up Comic, both were on the
boat. And the ark was full, but more was to come and they coming still. Ethel
Waters was on the ark, Octavia Butler, hip good, up upon this boat. Slinger
Francisco, robed in African wax print and dancing as man, Eric Williams,
dead and living same time, also wrapped in kente. Larry Lee, masked and
southern drawling, Fats Waller, Art Pepper, Miss Bobbye Hall, Gang Gang
Sara, blown from Guinea to Les Coteaux Tobago, who climbed the great
silk cotton tree in Culloden with intentions to fly back to Africa, but fell to
stony death because she had eaten salt, she was on the ark, as was The Mighty
Spoiler, The Mighty Terror, The Mighty Broclax, in proper soft pants, dead or
living among the dead, as taxi driver or stevedore, leaning into a cacophony
of whores. Pharoah Saunders and Yusef Lateef, Eric Roach was on the ark,
his book of poems still warm, under his arm, he did not drown, at least not
deeply, and when the ark had two days to go before it reach Southampton, here
come John La Rose and Charles Mingus, here come Paul Robeson and Beryl
McBurnie, even Olive Walke would rode upon that ark. This was years long
since the firearm ban, when the river washed down and cleansed the city, and
who eh drown waterlogged, and who eh dead, badly wounded, and the devil
come down with his escort and chariot to survey the land, and found poor folk
had hidden in holes in the earth and barrel sealed shut with laglee sap from the
breadfruit root and drowned: stupid-stupid. The poets had hid in trees. And
the devil rode on, and the houses of prime ministers were burnt to the ground,

and all round the embassy route, those grand facades and remnants of colonial times, were volcanically cast to ash and plundered. And the devil moved west, he was looking for that long throated woman who after making love one morning ventured him up to the hills overlooking the city, behind the bridge and the quarry, where his navel string bury, and show him his own city, laid out like a map before him, its grids, lay lines, the white foam foaming at the coast, so he went knocking at discotheque doors, but she was long gone upon the boat, with candle wax gripping her praying hands, making necromancy. Jan Carew was on the ark, and Dominique Gaumont, as was Milton Cardona and Rosetta Tharpe, Odetta, C.L.R. James, Kemal Mulbocus, but not Kamau Brathwaite, he was not on the ark, instead Baba, the great teacher had evaporated into air, into language, into sound, into the very sex fruit of poetry. Oil does not dry upon his tongue, nor honey on the tips of his fingers. But Spaceape was there, *yes, yes, yes, yes, yes!* Stephen Samuel Gordon was upon the bow. And the ark drove down to Bristol, Birmingham and Manchester too, it swooned to Alaska, New York, and Boston, Chicago and Philadelphia, New Orleans see it too, come now, Haiti, Cuba, Jamaica, Suriname, you bound to roam. Look, it pass through Aruba, Trinidad, and Grenada, it gone up the Orinoco river, and it never wear neck tie yet. It come up from the southern Caribbean all the way up to Pascagoula Bay. Yes, Spaceape was on the ark –
blowing
the big
ABENG!

ON WORK ROUNDTABLE

In 2013 we encountered a pamphlet-sized book published by *n+1* called *No Regrets*. It contained a series of conversations between different groups of women about the books that had formed them. Each discussion took the form of an edited transcript and was presented on the page as a dialogue, and although the format wasn't original, it felt new and important. The discussions were frank, unexpected and revelatory in the way only conversations between friends can be. Yet how rarely is the feeling – and the work they do in shaping us – of those conversations captured?

This was our starting point when it came to introducing a new feature to this magazine. We wanted to host a series of discussion on topics that feel pertinent to our times, around the subjects that dominate our lives and politics, and impact how art is made and books written. We wanted to ask those with experience the questions we were asking ourselves, questions like 'how did we get here?' or simply, 'how was it for you?'

This form, which we have called 'roundtables', blends the qualities of the personal essay and interview but aims to overcome the constraints of both. Instead of privileging only one voice, a number combine to share experiences and challenge each other. Informed but informal, led by anecdote and personal experience, we hope that each conversation will result in an unexpected and multi-faceted picture of the given topic – and inspire further conversations among readers.

Our first roundtable is on the subject of work, because how could it not be? The question of how we spend our days has never been more all-consuming or vexed. Over the past few years we have had to rethink everything we took for granted about work: getting paid, having a fixed place of work, the concept of leisure time, even the need for human beings in the workplace, when an app might do it better. But were we ever ready? As Joanna Biggs writes in *All Day Long*, her book on modern work, 'University had made us employable, but hadn't prepared us for work. The novels we had studied were about love and depravity; they weren't set in offices.'

Perhaps surprisingly, the participants in our roundtable didn't dwell on the technological advances that dominate headlines about work. Instead, they discussed the human aspects: commitment and sacrifices, care work and emotional labour, frustrations, disappointments and joy. 'Work is set against life, as if it were life's opposite,' writes Biggs, but 'as the days slide by, it changes us almost unobserved.'

ŽELJKA MAROŠEVIĆ   When you're at a party and somebody asks, 'What do you do?' how do you respond?

[Long pause]

ZYGMUNT DAY   I say, 'I work in construction' and then either they say, 'Ah, ok' and talk about something else, or they say, 'What do you *do* in construction?' and I say I install audio-visual systems. Sometimes they ask, 'What else you do?' and I say, 'Well I'm also a musician and I build recording studios as well.' Because I do those things. Then sometimes that's the interesting conversation and we take it that way, sometimes they want to talk about construction and we take it that way. So, it just depends. It depends on my audience, you know? I tailor it to my audience very much. In the pub I'm in construction... [Laughter]
JOANNA BIGGS   You never lie about it?
Z. DAY   No.
BIGGS   I try quite hard not to ask that question or to give that answer for a long time. I'm happy to talk about almost *anything* else, like the news or the weather or how they know the person whose party it is. Not because I'm ashamed of what I do but because it immediately places you in class terms, in money terms. It places you in a way that perhaps isn't helpful to having an interesting conversation at a party.
JON DAY   You do end up doing it, I think, however you try to avoid it. But I do feel a bit like, 'Fuck it, do I really have nothing more interesting to ask someone than what they do?' 'What gives you pleasure?' is quite a good one. [Laughter]
VICTORIA ADUKWEI BULLEY   I've never been asked that before.
J. DAY   Is that bad? Is that a bad question?
BULLEY   It's a good one, just nobody's ever asked me that before!

I'm getting better at saying that I write and I'm a poet, and right now that feels good because in between stable jobs I've had a lot of poetry-based work, like commissions or workshops. So right now it's fine because I can back it up and say, 'Yeah, I am because I do.' I like the simplicity of that because if you are really doing something, then why not say that you do that thing? You're not lying. But it's taken a long time to be confident in that because then the next question is, 'Oh, what kind of poetry do you write?' And it's like, 'I don't write sonnets.' You can't answer that question. 'What do you write

about?' 'My cat, sometimes... periods' and then the conversation is just dead.
BIGGS   What should you ask? 'Are you a poet, when did you last go to the Lakes?'
Z. DAY   Don't you think it's also hard to talk about it because it's not how you earn all of your money? It's not what you do all of the time. When I tell people I'm a musician, they always say, 'Oh, like full time?' What they want to hear is, 'Yeah! I'm on tour all the time.' But actually it's not your main job, or even your primary source of income. It's maybe not even what you do with most of your time. A lot of the time I'm not spending most of my time on it. I've also got to eat, you know.
J. DAY   Do you think people who respond in that way want you to answer, 'Oh, I'm a rock star, I'm on tour all the time' because it's a touch of glamour?
BULLEY   I feel like it might be the opposite.
Z. DAY   It's easier, especially in England – it isn't the same everywhere I've been – to say, 'Yeah, it's a bit shit, I'm having a terrible time, I'm not that good at it either.' [Laughter]
BULLEY   I've never been to America but I've met a lot of Americans who have said, 'That's amazing! That's great! Well done!' Here you have to be quite subtle and self-effacing. I get it but I also think we don't need to do that as much as we do. Why not say, 'Oh yeah, I really enjoy this'?
Z. DAY   In America they're good at it. When you say to someone, 'What do you do?' he'll say, 'Ah buddy, you know, I'm a poet.' You look on his Instagram and there's a picture of a cigarette with the words, 'She left the bed cold.' [Laughter] And then there's some British person over there who's written a fifteen-page sonnet sequence. They're amazing, but when you say, 'What do you do?' they respond, 'Oh you know, I work in admin.' It's an attitude thing, it's a lot about the English idea of knowing your station, knowing your place.
J. DAY   In Britain work is the toad that squats on your life in a kind of Larkin-esque way, whereas in America they seem to believe, 'I can find realisation, I can better myself and I can better my family's station by striving.' I mean, that's far too simplistic as a dichotomy.
Z. DAY   That's a weird thing: the idea that if you just work hard, you get good results. I've known it to be both true and not, in different types of work. For example, when I've been doing creative work and working really hard on it and it's been going absolutely nowhere. You can sense that you're get- ting better at it but the external bit of it that other

people see, that's not really happening. But then if you work really hard at your job, depending on what it is, you can actually get that result – where you get a pay rise and everyone's happy with you.
BULLEY   It's quantifiable.
Z. DAY   Exactly. That's also the thing about working in construction: the jobs are finite. We say, 'Right, we're going to build that' and then we build it, it's done. Whereas with creative stuff, you're slogging away at it for ages.
J. DAY   When I was a bicycle courier that was the best thing about it. The end of the day was the end of the day. I could leave it and I slept better than I have since because you've got nothing to worry about for the next day. You've just got to get up and do it all again. That was lovely.

SHIT JOBS; BIKE COURIERS; FASHION PEOPLE

MAROŠEVIĆ   Let's talk about the jobs that you've done just for money, not necessarily because you were particularly interested in them.
J. DAY   I was partly attracted to being a bike courier for that very reason. It's one of the few jobs that you could get physically exhausted doing, as far as I could tell. After leaving university I worked for three months at a TV company, which was just horrible. I hated being in an office and I hated people. I'm not a misanthrope but I didn't like teamwork and 'pulling together' and, you know, working with people, so I just felt, 'I need to get away from this.' I'd always liked cycling and actually it is badly paid and it's quite dangerous and it's not the sort of thing I'd want to do for the rest of my life. But I did also have one eye on the fact that it's quite a weird job and that I might write about it, so it became both a dead-end job but also an opportunity to write about something that other people didn't know much about.
MAROŠEVIĆ   Did you feel disingenuous among your colleagues?
J. DAY   No, because tons of people do that too. Loads of people write books about being a courier. So many couriers have other projects on the go, all of them are artists or photographers. All of them are photographers, because that's quite an easy thing to do when you're on the bike. You get your camera out and take a sunset photo of London Bridge or whatever. But the interesting thing about that job was that it also conjured up a sense of grassroots solidarity. There's no sick pay, you're just paid job

by job. About a decade ago, London couriers set up this thing called the London Courier Emergency Fund which is a kind of grassroots pay-out fund. They do fundraisers every now and then usually based around illegal road races. And then, if you're knocked off your bike, you get £60 a week to tide you over.
BIGGS   The earliest unions were exactly that.
BULLEY   After I graduated in 2013 I worked in a school as a teaching assistant. I loved being around young people and it was like being back at school – and I really enjoyed school.
MAROŠEVIĆ   Wow.
BULLEY   Honestly, it was sick! I'd be in class and a kid would crack a joke and I'd have to remind myself not to laugh, that I wasn't one of them any more. I almost went and taught. I had a place on a PGCE and I turned it down because I thought, 'I'm all of 23 years old, what do I have to teach?' So I did an MA instead. While I was doing the MA I worked at Leon. I would work from 6.30 a.m. at the King's Cross branch until 3.00 p.m. and then I would go from King's Cross to SOAS and print my work and then go home. It was gruelling. I only did that for three months but it was a long three months.
MAROŠEVIĆ   How many days a week were you working?
BULLEY   I would do three days a week. It was minimum wage and it was hard because when you're behind the counter, that's literally all you are. And people talk to you any kind of way. I remember one time I gave this woman porridge and it was meant to have blueberries and honey in it but I gave her banana and chocolate and she was so bitter about it. When I went to give her her money back she was like, 'No, keep the money. Just do better!'
J. DAY   Ugh!
BULLEY   And it really hurt because I didn't do it on purpose. It felt really hurtful. People talk to you, they're going everywhere. A lot of them are very wealthy. Fashion people were the worst.
J. DAY   Yeah, I found that when I was couriering. They were such—
BULLEY   They were the *worst*!
J. DAY   Was it freeing doing a job that's so unrelated to your poetry? The fact that you keep them so separate: this is what I'm doing for my money, and it doesn't take up any of my creative energies. Was that important to you?
BULLEY   Definitely, because I got a lot of ideas in the downtimes. Even if it's just cleaning tables, you

think, 'Oh this is an idea I've had and I need to write about when I get home.' Those ideas don't necessarily always come when you aren't doing that work.

Z. DAY   Occupy your hands and your brain has a bit of time.

BULLEY   Yeah, your brain does things. I think there's value in that work but that doesn't mean it's not hard.

MAROŠEVIĆ   When you were in these different work cultures, were you someone different? Did you find yourself behaving in a way that made you think, 'If my friends were here now, they'd say "What are you doing?"'

J. DAY   Definitely. It's such an anti-social world, the courier subculture. Firstly, you stink. You just sweat so much. You end up only hanging out with couriers because it attracts lots of people who can't work in other environments, either through choice or because they can't be employed for legal reasons. There are a lot of economic migrants. The courier companies are quite hands-off, they don't really give a shit who's doing their delivering and you don't need to have particularly good language skills, and you don't need CRB checks.

So it has assembled this ragtag team of misfits really. Also because of the nature of the work you're doing, to deliver a package quite quickly you have to ride like a bit of a dick and piss people off. It conjures up this sense of complete antagonism so that your only mates are people who are equally outsiders.

CALL CENTRES; KARL MARX; MCDONALD'S PARTIES

BIGGS   The scariest job I had was after university when I worked in a call centre. Every time you've called a call centre yourself you've known, 'This is a horrible thing. Why can't anybody talk in a normal way? Why can't anything get done?' But then when you're in it you somehow do believe in answering X number of calls in a certain amount of time. You do believe in it. [Laughter] I worked in two call centres. I worked in one where people rang up and paid their water bills. That was fairly easy, you were just trying to keep the volume down. The other one was in insurance for old people who'd crashed their cars. They'd call you up and tell you what had happened. That one was a lot more scary, there was a lot more of dealing with people in a weird situation.

J. DAY   Were you conscious of the fact that you wanted to be on the side of the people calling up? You know that thing about insurance – that if they say the wrong thing they won't get their money?

BIGGS   Yeah, I was. You were always dealing with slightly vulnerable people. But I also knew that that wasn't where I was going to end up for my whole life, I had other things I could go and do. I think that changed how I behaved. I could afford to be gentle, I could afford to do things how I thought they should be done. I knew this wasn't going to be where I ended up. Not because I disrespected it or thought that it wasn't a decent living but just because I wanted different things and I knew they were open to me in a way that they weren't for everyone else I was with. But it was exhausting emotionally.

J. DAY   Have you read that David Szalay novel *London and the South-East*?

BIGGS   No.

J. DAY   That's all about call centres and that work. It's really great. I mean it's sort of the sales side.

BIGGS   Which is different. At least with this you're giving some kind of service back. I interviewed someone for my book who worked in a call centre and the thing that was really affecting in the interview was that he kept on saying that what he hated most was never knowing if anything got finished. I think that happens a lot in the atomisation of work in these places. In the call centre, someone would come to me and say, 'I've crashed' and give me the details and I'd write them down. I'd never know what happened to that person next or if I'd fucked up by writing something, or not putting down enough detail. I think that's one of the things that is most difficult in modern work.

J. DAY   That's what Marx said about the alienation of labour, it's all about that. On a production line, for instance, you're only screwing in the one screw, you never see the finished car.

BIGGS   Imagine if in Leon you'd got to serve it *and* make it. Like that McDonald's party when you were little where you got to see behind the scenes. You were able to see how everything fits together, how the world works, the system.

BULLEY   Oh my god those parties!

J. DAY   That's one thing that's innately attractive about creative stuff. You're like, 'Here's the thing I'm making, here's me making it, I've made it, and here's me selling it or offering it to the world.' In his argument about alienation Marx talks about how selling the object is part of the enrichment it provides, both to the person who's selling it but also to the person who buys it. They can say, 'Oh that's an amazing poem, an amazing piece of music, an amazing spoon', or whatever it is, 'I can see that you're the person who created it.' That's why we have to create these ridiculous metrics in the modern workplace, abstract stars, the thing that lets you go higher and higher.

Z. DAY   I have to say I really get a lot of that in my job.

J. DAY   The satisfaction of finishing something?

Z. DAY   Yes, because someone shows me a design and they ask me, 'Can you build that?' I say, 'Yes. I can make that.' I make it and then at the end I show them how to use it. I get the process. I think that's why I've stuck with it for so long. I've done tons of different jobs but with this one I actually get a sense of achievement. In a way I think it distracts me from doing other stuff in my life, because it is almost like a creative process.

J. DAY   I think that's an important point because one thing I've always been slightly uncomfortable about is that it's clear that economic entrepre-neurialism is for some people a form of creative expression.

I remember going to Cuba about ten or twenty years ago and the relationship between private enterprise and the state was obviously so conflicted. The only food you could buy on the street was little pizzas, because I guess flour was less rationed than other things, with a basic tomato topping and this very strong, very sweet squash. And it was the same everywhere you went, it was almost McDonald's like in its uniformity. When I spoke to people the constant thing that they said dissatisfied them was the inability to create some sort of business. Not even in terms of a better life. Just...

BULLEY   Finishing something.

J. DAY   Yeah, as in, here's an idea I've had, can I make it work? You know everyone celebrates the romantic ingenuity of Cuban culture, the way they keep the cars running with bottle caps and whatnot but I think it puts into relief ingenuousness in an economic sense, which I really do think is... maybe I'm not a Marxist then... [Laughter] ... the creativity of capitalist endeavour.

'HOW LONG SHOULD SOMETHING TAKE?'

BIGGS   You're also talking about expertise, learning something, coming to something. One of the things I was just thinking about was when I was at the call centre the day was so different. As in, you clock in at a particular time because the computer knows if you're there or not, you get your break at a particular time and you're just counting, filling out that time so that you can have this weird coffee from the machine. I actually used to quite like that weird coffee. There are moments of respite but not many. You have a way of breaking up the day in a way that I don't any more.

Actually it's exactly the opposite in creative work, I don't know if you all find this, that's where you lose time! Like, 'Oh my god, I haven't washed for eight days' or 'I've been wearing this outfit for six days.' Work and time, learning how to manage time, is one of the skills of life.

Z. DAY   How long should something take? When I was at university there was a guy I was friends with who used to relentlessly read the Wikipedia pages of artists and say, 'By the time he was 25 he'd done that and that.' 'He was 21 when he did that, I'm 21.' You know, how long should it take? Creating stuff is so different because it might take one person a day to write a thousand words and it might take another person two weeks.

BIGGS   You have to respect yourself and know yourself a bit, and that takes time too.

J. DAY   Do you feel that working for the *London Review of Books* now is more akin to the clocking on, clocking off feeling you have with time? Or is it more akin to writing a piece or writing a book?

BIGGS   I have to be in the office because it's a bit like how you show up for anything. Like how you show up for your creative work. You have to be there to have the conversation that leads to the commission that leads to X happening. Sometimes it does feel a bit like clocking on and off but other times it doesn't, other times I find myself there really late and thinking about certain things. Also it blends into the rest of life way more than call-centre work. I'm thinking about it walking down the street, as I'm coming here, while I'm here, when I'm at home. So many friends work there so, you know, you don't stop thinking about it or talking about it.

J. DAY   Do you think that's a good thing?

BIGGS   Good and bad. It can get very claustro-phobic and scary. It can be nice to meet somebody who just doesn't give a fuck about the latest issue.

J. DAY   One utopian response would be, if we could live in a world without work we would just be writing poems and sitting round doing the things that we enjoy but actually—

BULLEY   I don't think we would, though!

J. DAY   No, exactly. The work is the work, in either scenario. It's hard to write a poem. Would you sit down by the tranquil bubbling brook in our fully automated luxury communist utopia and do that work? I don't know.

BULLEY   My partner often asks me, 'If you didn't have to work, what would you do?' I've always said I'd still want to be useful and have a role some-where. Even if it were some sort of utopian village, I'd like to be the woman who does *this*.

J. DAY   Say you don't need to do any of that? Say it was machines doing all that for you?

BULLEY   I'd still want to have a purpose.

CARE WORK AND EMOTIONAL LABOUR

BIGGS   What you're raising when you refer to 'the other sort of work' are the movements in feminism like 'Wages for Housework' and the idea of care work. As soon as you start saying, 'What if you didn't have to work as much, or as well, or at all?', I'm immediately thinking, 'Well I could do that for my mother, I could do that for one of my friends.' You know, instead of everything being rationed, things being squeezed into moments. I haven't got children but I have friends who have and you know that that child needs a little bit of extra time, someone to talk to them and explain things to them. It's that work which again doesn't end, which again isn't seen as really work, which again is also central to how society works.

MAROŠEVIĆ   Let's talk about care work. I think that's one of the things that has really changed in recent years – care work is being reclaimed as important and positive. Can you talk about your care responsibilities? And in your dedication to your paid work, what are you sacrificing? What is the care work that you could be doing instead?

J. DAY   I've been thinking about this a lot. Recently my girlfriend and I had a second child and it's wicked and lovely but also, at the same time, my girlfriend was made redundant from her job. She's always worked full-time and I work from home a lot. So there was this moment of crisis just before she went on maternity leave and now we've fallen into very traditional gendered roles in terms of how much care we provide. I got this weird manic obsession with us being impoverished and so I took on loads of work the week after my son was born.

I had this piece to write and I thought, 'Why the fuck am I doing this? I'm sitting in my office when my newborn child is downstairs.' I tried to get an extension and they said, 'Well, you can have an extra day.'

My girlfriend's obviously doing a lot more of the childcare than I am. I pat myself on the back sometimes when I wake up early and spend two hours with them at the beginning of the day to give her a lie-in. I think, 'Oh, I'm doing such an amazing thing', which is such a horrible feeling to reflect on – that it's just become a cliché of my own making. I'm not sure quite what the forces involved in that scenario are.

Z. DAY   Yeah, right. Is there a way out of it? That's the question you've got to ask.

J. DAY   Yeah there probably is because I don't need to be doing this labour and my girlfriend is going to find another job and everything's going to settle down into a more equitable share. It's amazing how that second child seemed to throw everything in the air and then it fell back down into this fifties cliché of man providing and woman doing emotional labour.

MAROŠEVIĆ   Did the two of you discuss what had happened – that you had fallen into roles you hadn't chosen for yourselves?

J. DAY   Yes. She is quite rightly saying, 'Well you don't have to. You're choosing to do this work.' I'm always saying things like, 'Oh, I've got to come to *The White Review* and talk about work...' Especially last year when I was judging the Booker Prize – even at the weekend I would say, 'I've got to read a novel today.' She said, 'After that's over your weekends are our weekends.' So we have had that discussion in a few different ways. It's usually about me feeling virtuous and then getting annoyed when she says, 'Actually, I do this every fucking day. Why are you so proud of yourself for spending two hours with your kids in the morning?'

BIGGS   It's funny that you called hers emotional labour and yours not because you obviously felt a pressure, which one might say was emotional, to provide more money for this burgeoning family, right? That is emotional labour. But that's different from care work. Sometimes people talk about having a relationship as emotional labour and I sort of think, 'Come on!' [Laughter]

J. DAY   So what is emotional labour? I thought it was the person who was always like obliged to send thank-you cards and pick up the pieces in a socially functioning family unit. Isn't that emotional labour?

BIGGS   I think it's like a Parisian waiter. He's doing his job perfectly fucking fine but he has contempt for you and he's allowed to have contempt for you. Emotional labour is someone telling you, 'Look, you have to smile.'

J. DAY   Right. So it's affect, projection.

MAROŠEVIĆ   But I thought it was also the way Jon defined it, of always being one step ahead of how someone will react to something or what someone will need.

J. DAY   In the scenario I just described then, you would say the emotional labour comes from the fact that I felt compelled to do this by some sort of emotion.

BIGGS   The actual labour of caring, who's changing how many nappies per day, or whatever, that would be care work for me. That's how I would distinguish it, otherwise it becomes super super gendered.

MAROŠEVIĆ   Yes, but I often find myself thinking about things in the office and then saying, 'No, I'm not going to be the one who thinks about this.' Like if it's someone's birthday, and also domestic things. So, who's going to wash the dishes or...

J. DAY   Make the coffee.

MAROŠEVIĆ   Yeah, exactly, make the coffee. So how do we define that? Is that care work in the office or is that emotional labour?

BIGGS   No, I probably would say that would be emotional labour. They do cross over slightly but I do think it traps women to gender all this stuff, to label all the traditionally female things as emotional labour, because I think men do know it, they do perform it. They also feel the pressure to be a certain way and happy in a certain role.

J. DAY   And that comes into the care work, doesn't it? Especially with children. You're obliged to be happy for your child. You don't want to say, 'This is fucking depressing and miserable'; 'I hate your stinky nappy, go away.'

Z. DAY   Yet a lot of people do experience that when they have a kid, right? Which is doubly hard because you've got your kid and everyone's going 'Oh, you must be having a wonderful time!' and you're like —

J. DAY   No, it's shit.

BULLEY   Really?

J. DAY   No! [Laughter]

BABIES; SYLVIA PLATH; JOY

MAROŠEVIĆ   I'm at a stage in my career where I'm surrounded by lots of amazing women who are very successful but I am aware that there is this gap, that there is a certain point when women do just disappear. I remember being in a conversation with two men I know and like and they were talking about a female journalist they admired and one of them said, 'She's not written anything recently. I wonder why not?' and the other said jokingly, 'Oh, she probably had a baby', and then they laughed. And there was such a sense of, 'Well, she's over for us now. We have nothing left to say about her.' I just wondered if you, I mean the women here, the men not so much, if it's something that you're aware of or worried about? Or have you found a way not to be worried about it?

BIGGS   I can definitely speak to this. I remember feeling very, very scared of the idea. I used to do the exact same thing, recall different people disappearing, people talking about them as if they were suddenly not serious about their career any more. I find the economics of it incredibly scary, especially if you don't have family help for it. This is so difficult to talk about it without it being really personal. I was married, there was a notion that we would and I know I pulled back from it entirely, finding it really scary. There were moments when we'd talk about it and I would say, 'Okay, what if we had a baby and you took it out for the morning and I wanted to write some fiction and I wrote two sentences. How would I feel when you came back?' I don't know if I'd have been able to handle that.

Subsequently, I've seen friends do it well. I don't think it's stupid to put your family life – if you really want it – first for a little while. I know that there are writers, Sylvia Plath was one of them, who really believed that you couldn't be a writer without having that experience of being a mother, of giving birth. I mean she used to be quite mad on those mystical things and interested in that experience.

MAROŠEVIĆ   There's an interview that Plath and [Ted] Hughes gave together for BBC radio. I've always found it quite sad. The interviewer says something like, 'What's daily life like for the two of you? Because you're both parents and poets. How strange!' and Plath says, 'Oh, for me it's very ordinary, you know, Ted goes out to work and I'm with the children and we go to the park and I'm just like all the other mothers and no one would know. Then sometimes I go home and sometimes I write.'

And it felt to me like such a covering over of her identity. But maybe she was happy like that, maybe she wanted to have those two different identities.
BIGGS   I could talk about Plath for a long, long time. I think she was at a cusp in time and history, the mid-fifties, early sixties, where those two ideas were in competition. Like not admitting that you're a writer and having to hide certain things. You can see it in her letters and her journals when you read them together – how much they're in conflict. And I feel that, and I don't really know what will happen to me, whether I will have children or not.

But I do feel like there's not that much room in the world. There are certain things that you're going to have to give up, that are going to have to be more important to you and the world is not going to help you, actually. It's very difficult. The only way I see it as possible is with some dude who gets it and also hopefully with women around you who are either mothers, aunts or friends. I just can't see any other way of getting through it, but then life is like that. You sometimes have to say, 'Fuck it! and let's see how it goes, and I might fuck up a bit, I might do bad things, it might go wrong.' What's the point of being alive otherwise?
J. DAY   The imbalance is that you're obliged to see these things in a different way to men.
BIGGS   It's doubly hard when you think your real work is happening outside of the work day. Then you know that that time will be taken up by a child, because they need you.
J. DAY   The kid occupies that position also. As in, the project outside of work could be the child or it could be the work, or both.
BULLEY   I think it's a shame that we hear these stories about women and think a woman with a child must have lost something or a part of herself. There are roles which women end up performing which are restrictive but then, at the same time, the experience of having a child is such a monumental thing that it should also be allowed to be a joy. I mean as long as it's on the mother's terms. Then what's wrong with that joy?
Z. DAY   You might get a great poem out of it.
BULLEY   I've read a lot of poetry written by women who are either talking about their children or the birth process, like Sharon Olds for example. The way they talk about motherhood, I think it's amazing. The only part of motherhood that scares me is the fact that right now at 26 I'm not earning enough to support a child. My partner likes his job but he's not a career person. He says he'd quite

happily stay at home and play with kids, and I believe him. And I'd quite happily be somewhere at a conference reading poems, and travelling the world. So I worry about providing in the masculine sense, that concerns me.

It almost happened for me last year. I found out I was pregnant in August and we miscarried just before eight weeks. It was really hard as I did not want to be pregnant. It was a complete accident. We both want kids but not right now. But we did decide to go ahead with it and there was a point when he said, 'You know as much as I'm scared, I'm impressed.' [Laughter] And it just seemed like a really guy thing. I dunno, is that a guy thing?
J. DAY   When my girlfriend got pregnant the sense of almost existentialist dread was lifted from me. It's pathetic, and it obviously occludes some profound psychological weakness on my part, but part of me was like, [deep voice] 'Procreation complete. Shutting down.'

LIES

MAROŠEVIĆ   There's an anecdote in your book, Jo, about your early days in London as a new graduate. After work you would sit on the floor with your flatmates and you'd all talk about work, your new workplaces, the details of it. I want you all to cast your minds back to those early days when you were first entering the world of work, when you'd graduated and were coming to it fresh-faced. What were your biggest surprises and disappointments about the world of work?
J. DAY   I was almost thirty before I had my first job, or experience of work in the way that you're describing. And it was strange to feel, 'I may be doing this for the rest of my life.' That was quite a strange feeling after so many years of isolation and drifting in and out.
MAROŠEVIĆ   I remember when I started my first job and my pension enrolment letter arrived in the post telling me when I would retire. It was on my birthday, like fifty years later. I just burst into tears. Seeing that date was so frightening – it was like someone had counted out my life and there was my end point. It was horrible.
J. DAY   What was the other part of your question, surprises?
MAROŠEVIĆ   I'll give you an example. I graduated and went straight into a job in publishing and one of the things that surprised me was that I had had such a romantic view of the literary

world and I just couldn't believe that some of the people I worked with weren't more enthusiastic and energetic about what they were doing. Because it seemed to me that if you weren't those things, why not go work somewhere where you could get paid way more money and care less? And it took me a while to realise that obviously people had been doing this job for many, many years and it's hard to keep up that enthusiasm. You have other priorities. But I remember being really struck by that and quite disappointed.

J. DAY   Are you still excited?

MAROŠEVIĆ   Yeah, I think I am. And I hope when I'm working with younger people now I do acknowledge their initial excitement and encourage it. But the other thing was that I was just so tired all of the time. [Laughter] And I really hadn't known about that. How tiring it would get! I remember on Friday nights just lying on the sofa and not understanding how it could be a party night, how people could go out on a Friday night.

Z. DAY   I graduated with a good degree in English Literature from Cambridge and I came out of it thinking, 'I fucking hated Cambridge, but at least now I can do a job, a really interesting job', and I just remember I couldn't find one. For a long time.

J. DAY   I remember that feeling.

Z. DAY   I was even going to interviews with companies like Bloomberg and they would always say at the end of the interview, 'Well thanks for this but we're not actually hiring at the moment' and then suggest I applied for their graduate scheme the next year. I'd go back to the flat I was renting with its single bed and think, 'I can't fucking eat. What am I going to do?' I remember feeling so pissed off with the system I'd bought into. I'd gone to university, I'd got this debt, I'd got this degree. I just thought, 'What's happened here?' I felt like I was wasting time, just wasting time. People would offer me a job – a three-month internship – and it paid maybe £1,000 a month and I was still fucked for money, I still couldn't really do anything.

A lot of my friends were doing really great stuff and I felt like I'd been left behind. Eventually I had to find something that paid better and was actually available – something I could walk into and they would say, 'We need you to start tomorrow.' That's how I found construction. I started as a labourer and now I'm a site manager. I've worked my way up in four years. I thought, 'I want to do something. I have potential but nobody wants it.' I found that

so frustrating. I was surprised because I was the only one from my school to go to Cambridge and while I was there I was noticing that life was very unfair – it was the first time I'd met people who were rich or posh, to be honest – and these people had such a big advantage over me already, and it was mostly those people who came out of Cambridge and got good jobs.

J. DAY   I remember that experience of looking through the jobs list at university. It looks as though there are jobs out there and you think, 'Okay. I'll apply for this, I'll apply for that, I'll do it methodically', but no one gets jobs like that.

BULLEY   No. It's a lie in a way.

Z. DAY   I mean, there were jobs. I was on the careers service. I used to go in every day and apply for all the jobs there were. You just didn't hear anything. It wasn't like they got back to you and said they had filled it; it was just nothing.

J. DAY   Some of the cynicism around the literary world – it's the only world I know, really – is that it's about who you know and having personal relationships with people. But when I think about how I have entered into that world as work, it is who you know but it's also how you get to know the people. You write to them, you write for them, Jo kindly takes you out to coffee... That's the work that is often invisible.

MAROŠEVIĆ   You're right, no one tells you about that work. You have to be quite canny to figure out that that's what's going on.

Z. DAY   It's obvious to everyone apart from those who don't know. That's what's heartbreaking. I had to say to myself, 'What are you going to do? Are you going to keep chasing this thing? Or are you going to start living your life?' The reason I can work in construction so easily and get on with all the blokes who are in that industry is because of where I went to school. I know how that environment works. Interestingly enough, what has allowed me to start doing creative work again is gaining the economic freedom you get from doing a job where you get paid alright money.

MAROŠEVIĆ   You've basically become your own parent in the way that the kids you were talking about had financial support.

THE ROAD NOT TAKEN; PORTFOLIO CAREERS

BIGGS   What strikes me about what you were saying about your work earlier – and this is where

I've gone wrong sometimes in parts of my life – is to think you have to choose either X or Y, A or B. Actually it's A but you can have a little detour through B. [Laughter] You can kind of have... I've had one thing at the *LRB*. I've worked there for twelve years, ever since I left university. And I've been very happy there. But recently I started my own sort of side-hustle – is that the word for it? – a small feminist press, and that has given me, one, different skills and, two, a completely different sort of vibe to a big established literary organisation. It's a bit more DIY, a little bit scruffier, a bit madder, a bit between friends and it's not supposed to make a massive profit. I was always really interested in what it would be like to start something. So sometimes you can tack things on at some point or have an experience that you can't quite have otherwise.

You know that Robert Frost poem, 'The Road Not Taken', with the two paths? You don't need to feel like that. You can do one for a bit and then move away from it and do something else. Like a woman thinking, 'Do I now have a baby, and how will that change my work?' Actually if we can allow ourselves to be more flexible, to let some things drop and then pick things up later, then maybe we would be happier.

MAROŠEVIĆ   I think all of you have stitched together careers formed of doing lots of different things at the same time. That feels like a very new thing in terms of work.

J. DAY   Portfolio careers. [Laughter] I think one of the benefits of having an identity as a writer is that it makes everything a potential subject. It gives a sense of continuity to either a portfolio career or the path-not-taken or these side tracks that Jo's talking about. A sense of coherence – that one day you might write the novel about setting up the press or write the brilliant satire on working in construction.

BIGGS   I also know there is no such thing as a full-time writer or a full-time musician. You look back on people's careers and you realise, 'Oh they had a small press for a couple of years', or, 'They were a mother'; 'They were teaching.' There's this great *In Our Time* on Aphra Behn and they talk about how she moved from plays, when plays suddenly didn't pay very much, into a novel, and then she moved back. Actually there's always been movement. If you're interested in telling stories then you're interested in the world so you don't necessarily want to do the same thing all the time.

J. DAY   It's also a dangerous thing. The idea of everything as a potential subject is quite sad in some ways. Or it prevents you from fully experiencing it, because you always have the potential to flog it to someone. It goes back to that question of what you would do if you didn't have to work – you could go on an adventure, sail around the world... But all of the things I think to do, I always think, 'Would that make a good book? Would that be an interesting thing to write about?' There's no concept of leisure when you think, 'This might be cool to write about.'

BULLEY   Would you go somewhere that you didn't see as an interesting place to write about?

J. DAY   Well, that's why you end up going to quotidian unlikeable places because you're more interested in the writerly aspect of them. I guess what I mean is that there is some sense of curtailment. I'm not saddened by it particularly, only when I reflect on it. There's nowhere kind of pure.

MOTHERS AND FRIENDS

MAROŠEVIĆ   Can you talk about what it's like to work with friends or mothers or people who aren't the usual colleagues one would have?

BULLEY   I don't speak my parents' language, which is Ga, one of the many Ghanaian languages. They both speak it, they just didn't teach us. I came to a point where I felt as a poet, 'Words are all I have', and I feel very limited only to have mastered one language. Even if I have fragments of other languages I can't 'poet' in those languages, so wanting to know my parents' language led me to think, 'Why not employ my mum as my translator and knowing what my poems are saying will help me to become more familiar with the language.' Then I thought, 'Actually there are quite a few other poets I know who have these other languages in their heritage or in their households', so I thought, 'Why don't I just make a project where I include them and get their mums to translate them? And have both of them filmed – so have the mother reading the translation, the daughter reading the original – and also have an interview between them?' That's basically what *MOTHER TONGUES* is.

It's something that really interested me – to see things translated back rather than forwards. As in, when something is translated into English, people say, 'It's open to the world!' I kind of want to go against that because a lot of those languages are dying out. I also don't believe that monolingualism is the best thing for mankind.

MAROŠEVIĆ   When you were working with your mum were the two of you communicating in a way different to usual? Did it feel like it was your space you were bringing her into?

BULLEY   It felt like she was a collaborator. It was really nice because we were in a studio and I was saying, 'So now read it like this, do it again but read it as though you're telling a story.' So I felt like I was a director and she was an actor. It changes the dynamic and you see your mum in a different way. I think that's a really important thing as in that space she wasn't just my mum, and that was liberating for me.

J. DAY   Had you seen your mum in a work context before?

BULLEY   I mean she's a midwife so she's taken me to the hospital and I've met her colleagues, but not *at* work, like her working.

MAROŠEVIĆ   Jo, can you talk about working with friends?

BIGGS   One thing I've found really wonderful is how they're the only ones who get it. When something tiny happens they really, really get it. And that is really cool. I think I've found it useful because I was having a hard time working: I wasn't really writing and I didn't know what projects to do, but I found having to show up for my friends incredibly good for getting back into work, and I don't think I would have been able to do that without them. At the time I needed a bit more support around work and they gave that to me in all sorts of ways. I could let go as I felt held, I trusted them.

MAROŠEVIĆ   One thing I've found working with friends is I allow myself to be way more vulnerable than I would be with colleagues. And because of that it's allowed me to address things, decide how I feel about certain things, or ask questions if I don't feel confident about something. When you first start working you don't know anything so you're just trying to catch up and then you get to a point where everyone assumes you know everything, so you can never go back and ask. Whereas with friends you can do all of that.

BIGGS   One of my experiences – I feel like that's entirely true for me – when I got to the workplace I was a little bit giddy, a little bit fresh, and I remember it being clear to me that I had to tamp all that down. It wasn't clear to me that I could be myself. I felt there was a way of doing things and I had to learn it, and I think that's right actually, that's right as an initiation. The tone of the *LRB* should

not be an excitable 24-year-old. It should be a serious tone. I went wrong a couple of times at the beginning and they were really painful to me. I can still remember them. But it was good as I needed to learn that you don't do that – you are a professional, you're not just a nice girl helping out at the *LRB*.

WORK IDENTITIES: MERITOCRATIC BUILDING SITES

J. DAY   I'm struck by how both of you think about the communal endeavours of working in an office or with other people. I'm surprised by how psychologically interesting and important it seems to have been to both of you. It's not something I feel I've really ever had in a job. I feel like all the jobs I've done have been not lonely, but you do your thing and no one else is really part of it.

MAROŠEVIĆ   I feel that it's completely tied into how I think about myself. Do you feel like that too, Victoria, that it's very mixed in?

BULLEY   I think I can get tired of myself. I do like my own space and my own time, being a bit of a loner in a way, but I think that there's a point where I do need to bounce off other people. I think I like a bit of both. I wouldn't want to be in an office all week with the same people but I might need a bit of that to add structure so I can tell what's me and what's not me as well.

MAROŠEVIĆ   To return to what Jo was saying, what's everyone's identity at work? Can you be yourself?

Z. DAY   I'm a version of myself for sure. It's a weird one. For one thing my work is a bizarre environment. You've got a Polish bloke, a Nigerian bloke and three guys from Romford, and all of these people somehow have to gel and do this thing together. But one thing I would say about the idea of appropriateness is that upsetting people is not very much at the forefront. [Laughter] You're not very policed in terms of how you interact with other people. It's a very, very diverse industry and although it's overwhelmingly male, it's not only men and ethnically it's very mixed. People from all over the world work on London building sites. It's nice in a way as there's a certain amount of respect people have for each other but there's also a lot of tension.

MAROŠEVIĆ   Between who?

Z. DAY   Well between white working-class people and Polish people, for example. That is a tension that exists. Between management and worker, and between different people doing different jobs at the same time in the same place. You have to be diplomat in a lot of instances. You've also got to be quite tough and really assertive, like you have to be able to have an argument with somebody. But on building sites people aren't very judgmental; you're only judged on how well you can do the work. It is very meritocratic in a certain sense. The question is more, 'Can you do it? Can't you do it?'

That's almost why I like it as you don't really have to worry about all that stuff. Builders do have a bit of a reputation as being a bit un-PC and I think they are, that's correct. But I also think it doesn't necessarily come from a bad place. It's more like: if you were working with all these different people all the time it would be very hard to have in your head, 'Okay, I've got to say that to him, that to him.' The easiest way to deal with it is just to confront it head on and take the piss out of each other, do you know what I mean? It's quite hard to get used to at first as I came out of university and that's a very politically correct environment, and then you get thrown into this other environment which is not. But in that way it's meritocratic – everything is up for grabs.

'I'M REDUCING THE AMOUNT OF WORK I'M OFFERING FOR FREE.'

MAROŠEVIĆ   Have any of you had mentors?
J. DAY   I think, in a writing context, editorial relationships can be so fruitful and important. Jo's my mentor really, when it comes to writing and thinking about pieces and having a relationship with an editor over time and learning both what they like, but also how they approach writing. Those people can be your peers as well as your elders, maybe.
BULLEY   In terms of literature it didn't really occur to me that there were people who would take an interest in your work actively and say, 'Are you applying for this?' or, 'Have you thought about that?' That didn't occur to me but it has been very important for me. When I did the Barbican Young Poets programme meeting Jacob Sam-La Rose, who runs that, changed what I thought mentorship was. For me it's just been someone saying, 'You're capable of this' or, 'Why not?' It's been as simple as that, which is great because it means I know I could mentor. I know I could mentor my friends and they

mentor me because it's really more encouragement than... you're not giving someone anything, you're just saying they can do it.
MAROŠEVIĆ   Is money important to you all? When you create work in which you've invested so much of yourself, how do you put a price on it? And how hard is it to say, 'This is what I deserve for this work?'
J. DAY   I suppose money didn't mean anything to me until we had a child and now we have a mortgage. Now I know I at least have to earn enough per month for those obligations or we'd be homeless. And every now and then when I calculate if I was sacked from King's if I could go back on the bike and earn enough doing that or writing, I think we could almost do it. And I feel thankful for the possibility of that safety net.
MAROŠEVIĆ   I guess another questions is, do you feel secure in what you are doing? For example, I got fired from my first job when I was 16 because apparently I was too chatty...
J. DAY   That's not a sackable offence!
MAROŠEVIĆ   But it's funny because I've kept that fear with me ever since and I'm still afraid of being fired. I'm also afraid of what would happen next. I feel like there is no safety net.
J. DAY   Do you think that's just something they make us feel?
Z. DAY   I don't know, I've experienced it directly, having no money. I definitely have had points in my life where I've thought, 'How am I going to pay that bill?' I never feel totally secure, especially living in London. In my early twenties I felt like the economy was crushing me. And I'm only just getting out of that now.
BULLEY   One thing I've been experiencing a lot is just getting used to asking to be paid.
ALL   Yeah.
BULLEY   And I've realised how doing that has actually helped me to enjoy the work I do so much more. If someone's putting in a request for your work and they say, 'Unfortunately we don't have any funds to pay you but it's a great platform', I've come to a point where I made a project and did everything myself. I don't need a platform. I contacted a producer at *Woman's Hour* and got me and my mum on the programme. I didn't need a platform to do that, I just did it myself. I've been turning some things down and not saying, 'I can't afford to do this' but, 'I'm reducing the amount of work I'm offering for free.' Ironically the work I've been getting requests for since that transition

has paid more. So I don't know if it's the universe saying, 'Oh, you want money, do you?'

'HOW DID WE GET INTO THIS MESS?'

MAROŠEVIĆ   As I was preparing these questions and thinking about work, I realised I was approaching the topic from the angle of, 'How did we get into this mess?' I feel we've got to a point with work where you think, 'What the fuck's going on? Why aren't we getting paid for things? How did internships happen? Why are there so many working families living in poverty?' Do you all feel like the system is broken?

J. DAY   What's really sad about London, and indeed Britain, is the degree to which it is limiting the kinds of projects and work being made. It goes back to the question of identity we were discussing at the beginning, I mean the work we want to identify ourselves as doing and the work we are obliged to do to pay for that. It's limiting the first of those two possibilities. I watched that film *Victoria* last night – you know the German film shot in one night?

MAROŠEVIĆ   That's a great film.

J. DAY   It's kind of amazing. They did it in like four takes. And this was a bunch of young film makers in Berlin, who produced this incredibly intricate and difficult and beautiful piece of work, and I don't think that could happen in London. I don't think you could get that many people able to offer their labour for free or for no money essential-ly, which is probably what that film depended on.

And I think the question of cross-subsidy shouldn't be... We now talk in terms of the work we get paid for doing and that's an important step. The only way people can operate in the contemporary economy is around those questions. But the alter-native is perhaps one we shouldn't discount either, which is that life should be cheaper and we should create space for doing free work around the things that we're interested in... I don't know... This idea of the degree to which you have to professionalise yourself quite early on in a creative degree now— it strikes me that you are potentially limiting the kind of work that's being made.

BIGGS   Exactly. People need to be paid fairly so they can live. I mean, money isn't the most important thing to me either but I need to be able to get by. Sometimes I think I wouldn't want to be paid more or less but I would like more time. You're

exactly right: we need more space in our lives to do the things in our life that we really want to do for free.

MAROŠEVIĆ   Final question: where do you see yourselves in five years' time?

[Laughter. Long pause.]

J. DAY   I feel like I never want to apply for another job again.

SANAM KHATIBI

PLATES

ART

JONAH
JOHANNA HEDVA

FICTION

After *The Eliza Battle*, I went to Berlin to recuperate, to nurse my pride. I had been there many times at that point, since first visiting in 2005 when I was part of a group show, and it had become my place for retreat when L. A. started to feel monstrous, as it regularly did; I'd been part of several group shows over the years and then there was a major museum biennial thing in 2011; there were meetings with curators arranged for the months of December and January; and I was also supposed to see a few gallerists who wanted to represent me, had been inviting me for months, more fervently after news of this last show; I had friends I could stay with, and sublets of people out of town, the Berlin way, a city of transience, expatriates, refugees, and nomads, but I rented a flat for myself, in a different part of town than most of the people I knew; and in the cab from the airport, I started to fall asleep, head nudging the window, I hadn't slept on the flight, it was nearing 4 p.m. Berlin time, the sky was steely; and I was able to make out the brown buildings with their box balconies, the typography of the street signs, the black coats being dragged around by little moons of grim faces, the Muslim women in their headscarves and long dresses that dusted the ground as they walked, and I felt at home.

I hadn't spoken to or seen Hanne in the month or so between the opening and when I left. Cal had, as expected, texted many times, beginning on the night of the opening, wondering where I'd gone, if he could come over later, and something the next morning, 'you were so radiant last night, lover.' Then the texts started to end in question marks, a flurry of them for a few days, but by the time I'd made it to the airport, they'd stopped altogether, and I'd already started to forget the features of his face.

By the time I arrived at my flat in Mitte, the posh part of town, it was completely dark, and I found that the heater hadn't been turned on. The rooms felt like a morgue. I switched on all the lamps, remembering the difference of German light switches from American ones, a rounded, phallic little knob instead of a flat geometric angle, but the weary light only made the place seem more like a tomb, filled with a cold that had been living there, undisturbed, for a long time, and wasn't about to vacate for me. I called the landlord, no answer. Left a message as I flicked off the lamps, and gave up to being claimed by the rules of the place. I fell into bed with all my clothes on, my coat, gloves, scarf, and hat, and slept hard. I awoke a few times in the night, stiff and frozen, my eyes parching where the lids met. I stayed in bed, curled like a pill bug, until the light started to leak through.

I took a bath, holding the showerhead on its silver leash over my forehead and shoulders, getting warm only where the sprinkle of water hit. The bathroom was newly renovated, as was the rest of the flat, in the jail-cell chic of German design, with slate floors and walls the colour of wet cement. There was a fresh bar of soap, brown and angular, shaved off a block that smelled loamy and ripe, like wet wood, but the tinny smell of the tap water rinsed everything, and the cold killed all the steam. I went out for breakfast, to sit somewhere and get warm, maybe I'd go to my favourite indoor swimming pool later. My meetings didn't start until the next day, or maybe tomorrow; I had a little time. The sky was the colour of the walls of my flat, and mild spasms coursed up and down my neck from its being chilled for so long. *The Eliza Battle* had sold out, and I had some money, more than usual, although I've always been bad with money, either having none until I have some again, or having a lot and then, just as quickly, none again, never a plan for how to stabilise the rise and fall of it, someone once told me that this trait was because I grew up not only poor but raised by addicts, trained to live as though each day is the culmination of all days, always seeking the rise, always living in the fall, so with my bit of *Eliza Battle* money, however much more it was than usual, I went to a swanky brunch place that served plates of sliced cheese with a cluster of grapes for 20 euro, which my friends, who all lived in Neukölln and Kreuzberg, despite having solid careers and plans for their money, would hate me for. Five years ago, I would have hated me too, but I had my justifications, my ego. Later, I would call my friend Yves, who lived in Neukölln, a Frenchman descended from Martinique-born grandparents, I'd known him for many years, since we were in the same show together in 2007, then again in that museum thing, he was the person I called my best friend, even sometimes my soulmate, but first I needed coffee, the cold had started to feel like loneliness, like I'd lost a long race that I'd been determined to win.

'Is it *you*?' Yves's voice, cool and low, gave away his smile.

'God,' I said into the phone, 'it already *sounds* like you're not on the other side of the world.'

'So,' he breathed, 'my wife, you have arrived. And how is it in your chichi headquarters?'

'The heater's broken, apparently, says the landlord. I've been sitting at a café all day just to keep warm. Can I come to yours tonight?'

'Of course – should we have a party?'

'Not yet.'

'You know where it is. Come whenever. I'm working, of course.'

'I'm just going to swim at the pool first.'

'Ha, yes, of course. Have fun, mermaid.'

When he opened the door, his large hands enveloped my head. 'Your hair!' he said, kissing my face. 'You look like a little boy!' He stepped back, leaning his thin, ropy frame on the door, grinning, his body was graceful and his hair had grown; it curled around his ears, sticking out in dense coils of blackish brown that I noticed was the same colour as the soap in my bathroom. There was a lot of grey in it now. I hadn't seen him in two years. 'It's so good to see you,' he said, curving his frame to the door like a ballerina on her bar, 'even if mermaids can't have hair like this.'

The lambent light in his apartment bronzed his mahogany skin, his loose burgundy clothes, and I could smell his cedar cologne merging with the odour of food. His apartment was warm and lit by candles, the heater hissing reliably, like a big hibernating animal, and I could hear Nina Simone's regal sadness being voiced in a room somewhere. I wanted to cry from the swelling gladness in my throat. Returning. He started to talk, taking my coat, moving into the kitchen, bringing out the wine. I'd always loved his voice. It was deep, like a cello, and he spoke British English through his French accent, which made him sound elegant and always a little disdainful. He folded his long frame into a chair, stopped talking, and lit a cigarette, letting his onyx-coloured eyes rest on me for a while. We could go for long periods of easy silence and gentle looking, and I nestled into my chair, smoking too, and returned his gaze.

I put out my cigarette. 'I had an extraordinary experience at the pool today, I have to tell you,' I said. 'In the showers, there was a woman, very large, doughy. Lumpy and pale, one of these German ladies – '

' – salty pillars of the earth,' he said, making his shoulders big and clenching his neck.

'Yes. Like the colour of chicken broth. She had that grey-blonde hair, that *un*-colour, you know? And she kept her back to us the whole time. She never showed her front, even as she went out, she pulled her towel around her, waddled out of the stall, like a big baby. On her back, on the left side near her shoulder blade, was a scar – but, like, an *intense* scar, Yves. I've never seen anything like it, I couldn't stop staring at it. It was like a whole chunk of her had been scooped out. It was the size –' I looked around for a piece of fruit, then held up my fist '– like this big!'

'The size of the fist is how big the heart is, you know,' Yves said, making his own fist. I saw his fingernails were painted blood-red, as dark as the wrinkles of his knuckles.

'Yes,' I nodded. 'It was like her heart had been scooped out of her, but from the *back*. Like they had gone in from behind, when she wasn't looking – or she'd asked them to do it that way, because she couldn't handle it from the front. There was another woman in the showers who was staring at it too. I caught her, and she looked away. I had a thought – ' I paused, feeling a crease in my memory, ' – I don't know. I don't know. I, I wanted to lick it.'

'Lick her scar?'

'Yeah. I know, I know. It was so smooth and shiny, but it was also, just, so – I don't know – *empty*.'

'Didn't you just have your birthday?' Yves got up, went to the stove, stirred something in a pot.

'33.'

'Like Jesus.'

'And so you're almost 40?'

'Ten more days.'

'Are we having a party?'

He placed a bowl in front of me, and one for himself. They were the size of dinner plates, dirty colours of earthy blues, and I recognised the rough hand-made grit of them. 'Did Alain make these?' I said.

'Yes. The only good thing I got from him, probably.' We brought spoons to our lips. The broth had oily clusters of gold drifting on the surface.

'Yves, this is delicious,' I said. I wanted to cry again.

'Yes, I'd like to have a party. But I was thinking – my place is so small, and I have work everywhere for the show in February.' He trailed off, refilling my wine.

'You want to have it at mine?'

'You always know what I'm thinking.'

We clinked glasses, and finished our dinner with sporadic speaking. The music from the other room reached its end. He waved me away when I tried to do the dishes, pushing me into the living room, where we sat, finishing the wine, on the sofa he'd reupholstered with the grey wool Swiss Army blankets of one of his heroes, Joseph Beuys.

'I can tell,' he said, on our fifth or sixth cigarette, 'that you've had a heartbreak.'

'God,' I groaned. 'Let's not talk about it.'

'But you made work about it, I presume. I *hope*.'

'But it didn't help. The opposite, actually.'

'That's the risk, always.'

'No, not like that. It's just – ' I saw then, like a phantom had risen in front of my eyes, that the dilution I'd hoped Berlin would give me from Hanne had not yet happened, and even worse, was working more like an attrition '– I'm worried it's only the beginning for me, but I'm the last one to the party.'

'Ah,' Yves started to chuckle. 'You've fallen for a slut. *I* see.'

'You know I hate that word.'

'Yes, but it's different for me.'

'Why, because you're a man?'

'Of course, my love – that's *always* the reason, isn't it?'

We both laughed at this, but mine was limp. Yves went on to tell me about his new love, a young Adonis, white, twinky, named something like Timmy or Timo, a dancer, perfect shoulders, hung, but I had floated away, my mind flipping through images, Hanne in ropes, Hanne standing over me, Hanne and Cal's tongues in each other's holes, and then the woman at the pool, her heart being dug out, I imagined with a long spoon, like the kind that Berlin cafés give you with your latte, then I thought, or maybe she had been shot, and they'd had to tunnel into her to get at the bullet, I gulped the last of my wine, saw the woman on her soft, big stomach in bed at night, nightgown undone, the hole in her back stinging, the bandage sticking to it, and then, when it had healed into the shiny, concave pit, how a nose, a tongue, a gentle fist, would've fit there perfectly, when Yves touched my knee, and said: 'You're tired, you should sleep.'

I agreed with him, and let him lead me into his bedroom.

'Aren't you coming?' I said, as he turned to shut the door behind him.

'It's Berlin, remember. We're nocturnal, you barbaric American.' A sound-less laugh jumped in both our shoulders. 'I'll try not to bump you when I crash in here at dawn.'

'Bump me all you want,' I said. 'Love you.'

He shut the door, and we were alone. I spread out on the bed. The room turned slowly, and I felt like I might vomit, so I turned on my side, and hung my head halfway off the bed. The next thing I knew, I heard the click of the bedside lamp being turned off, and saw Yves's sinewy, dark chest and wiry arms folding back the covers in the dawn light. He burrowed into the bed, and I heard him sigh. The trace of stale cigarette smoke was all that was left of his cologne. In the colourless light, I saw that the skin on his face had sunk into the cheeks. He looked much older, grey in his stubble too. I thought of when we'd first met. I had been 24, 23, or so, it was the opening for the group show, one of the first I'd ever been in, and the first I'd been in 'internationally', I'd made it into something important enough that I needed to fly to Berlin and conduct my inclusion in person, although now, of course, I sent work all over the globe to be in group shows and paid them little attention, marked them on a calendar, collected the cheques, Yves had looked dashing in that room, on that first night, wearing a purple suit and hot-pink sneakers, the only black man in the room, and he'd said so, noticing me, the only yellow person, as we snuck out early to drink in a Turkish-owned bar, 'They only wanted me because I'm black,' he'd said, 'and gay, too, ha, two minority birds with one rock, is that how you say?' and later that night, both too drunk, falling on each other, he wept, his face disfigured with sobs, for many reasons, none of which he explained out loud, finally bowing his head to apologise, 'I don't even know you,' he'd said, 'though I feel strangely like I do,' he was the age I am now, 33. Like Jesus.

Soon he was snoring lightly, a lowing rumble in his dipped chest and throat. I pulled the curtains closed and the room was shadowed a sooty violet, like a bruise. I felt a tingle in my vagina. Went to pee and felt a burning. Held his shaving mirror between my legs and saw that I was swollen and bright red. Must have been the pool, or the plane ride. Or the drinking. I don't know. My shoulders drooped. So much for fucking her out of my mind. I hobbled to the kitchen, underwear around my knees, found yoghurt in the refrigerator, and scooped with my fingers, pushing it into myself as far as I could go.

After my meeting with the first gallerist, during which I was hungover and said little, we had some people over to mine. The heater had been fixed. As dinner parties do in Berlin, it started around 9 p.m., the food served after a couple of hours. Yves and I cooked together, both wearing long robes he'd brought out from his closet, his a faded charcoal linen, and mine magenta silk. We indulged in selfies, which he posted to Instagram with the caption, 'My queen came home.' I was so happy I didn't check how many likes we got. He invited his Adonis, whose name was Theo, to come early to help with the cooking, and our mutual friends, all artists, living in Berlin, but of course from somewhere

else, with steady careers, facing their mid- or late 30s by drinking more expen-
sively, spending more money in general, making their plans for it, trying to
feel comfortable in their power by performing a confidence of accepting it, as
though it were the natural order, that they deserved it, however strange it felt,
the performance seemed to make up for the hesitation, or at least moderate the
anxiety, which meant that all the wine they brought was quite good, something
we'd have sneered at in our 20s, but felt inwardly proud of as we fingered the
stems of our glasses and drank bottles. There was Tamás, perhaps the most successful of us, Hungarian, who'd been making sculptures out of Styrofoam and
marble, layered together in thin slices, modelled on the Ancient Greek *Kouros*
statues of nude young warriors, but with the faces of current celebrities; he'd
shown this work in the Whitney Biennial some years before, and had just leased
a large warehouse studio, which he filled with bustling assistants and models for
larger-scale commissions; he brought a woman named Celeste, originally from
New York, who had brassy golden skin, and called herself a 'mutt', 'you know,
post-racial', and everyone laughed, she had the smallest hands I'd ever seen; she
said she made videos about colours and capitalism, I saw a phone go around
showing an image splintered into many shades of beige; there was Agata, from
Poland, who made her work in the empty, ruined buildings of former warzones,
where she'd broadcast radio shows, or make and screen 16 mm films; she had
tightly curled, dyed black hair, shaved over her ear, and swept to the side by a
long clip of mother-of-pearl, and lipstick the colour of carbon; she'd once sat for
me, an almost-muse, during a summer I'd spent in Berlin in 2010, when I was
reeling from my longest relationship ending, but I was too fickle to commit my
obsessions to anyone in those months; she came alone, wrapped in a camel-hair
coat and black leather gloves and looked like an oryx; there was a couple I'd met
last time I'd been here, Jack and Clemens, American and Dutch, respectively, who made abstract De Kooning-esque paintings and abstract Martin-esque
paintings, respectively, and who I had little respect for as artists, maybe because
so many others did, popularity has always made me sceptical, but who I enjoyed
as people; they were more Yves's friends than mine; they brought with them
a man, I assume, intended for me, whom I'd heard of, an artist who'd recently
exploded in New York, and had come to Berlin for his first solo show here, last
September, and had decided to stay for a while; he kept his black scarf on the
entire evening, I could tell it was cashmere, and that this was why he kept it
on; his new money; I thought his name was Jonah, and I called him that a few
times, until Yves pulled me aside, and whispered, 'His name is Dominic, what's
the matter with you?' We both laughed into our palms; I was uninterested, my
vagina full of yoghurt and infection, my head thudding with images of Hanne
but soon they were draining away, pooling into the conversation, the swell of
laughing, the toss of minor disagreements that gave way to long monologues
of opinion; the conversation frothed at one point when Jack, the De Kooning
mooch, asked Yves what he thought about all these black artists getting shows

all at once and didn't it make Yves proud, 'Like how you are proud when Pollock is given another retrospective?' Yves said, and Jack started to exhale in puffs but Clemens cut in with, 'Aren't Americans cute!' and we all contrived a laugh. Most of the questions directed at me had to do with L. A. gossip, the art scene's new stars and recent washouts, the nepotism and incest; who had slept with whom and for what, whose Instagram had somehow just passed 20,000 followers, whose drug problem was getting out of control, who had given up the last, or first, bits of their integrity, how bad, really, was the piece, and how much did it sell for; which city had what; and what, of course, it didn't have; would it ever get it? Probably not. At some point after dessert, Yves and Theo disappeared into the bedroom and Agata pulled out her tarot cards; everyone turned their attention towards her as she held up her ornamented hands to tell their futures and pasts; relieved, I went out on the balcony, wrapped in a blanket, to smoke.

It was late, 2 or 3 in the morning, maybe later. I didn't have a watch. There was a light on in the apartment across the courtyard; I could see straight inside, no curtains against the naked glass. I saw a woman, white, older, skeletal, with grey hair fuzzed out around her head like a ball of dust, on her knees in her living room. She was turned away from me, and wearing a robe, the same colour as mine, fiercely pink, the same lush fabric. I looked down at my own garment to check; yes, they were exactly the same. She was digging, with a small spade, into a huge earthenware pot of dirt, the size of a washing machine, in front of her. She wore gardening gloves, her back hunched over her work; she looked like she was kneading dough. She put the spadefuls of dirt into a pile next to her, but I couldn't see if she was depositing them into another container, or onto the floor. I watched her for a while, feeling the prickling in my scalp awaken the sting in my cunt. Sometimes, she stopped to rest, sitting back on her heels and wiping her forehead with her sleeve. I couldn't see her face. I tried to will her to turn around.

'There you are,' a noise cut into me. I turned, startled. It was Jonah.

'Mm,' I said. I turned back to my woman, but the light had gone out. She was gone. I blinked.

'What are you looking at?' He slid next to me, lit a cigarette.

'There was,' I was confused, I pointed into the dark. 'Uh, there – there was a woman there, in her apartment, digging in the dirt.'

'Dirt?' he looked out on the black building, brought his cigarette to his lips.

'Yes, on the floor of her living room. She had a huge pot of it.' I searched the façade of the building, forgetting now which window had been hers. They all looked the same, still and black.

'It's kind of late, don't you think, to be gardening in your living room?' I could hear the bemused disbelief in his voice, his method of flirting.

'Whatever, I saw her,' I snapped, turning to look for chairs on the balcony. I found none, so I leaned against the door, away from him.

He held his hands up, 'Okay, okay,' and I saw he had a silver watch on his wrist. Its large face glinted at me, impudent, wanting too much already.

I said nothing.

'Hey, I heard great things about your last show. Very visceral. *Abject*, even, was what my friend said. He was there. Sexy, he said, but in a fucked-up way.'

The silence hung.

'So, yeah, congratulations,' he said.

'Thank you.'

'No, really. I'm not eating your ass,' he said, taking a step closer. Don't say it, I thought, don't you fucking say it. 'At least, not yet.' Oh god. *Fuck* this. I let out a retching sound and crashed inside, storming past the fortune-telling, to the bathroom, whose door I slammed and locked. I sat on the toilet, pulling my chalky underwear off, and felt my cunt throbbing with distaste. I turned on the shower, and stayed in there, under the hot spray, for as long as I thought it would take until they were all gone. I rubbed my body with the wood-soap, used its weak lather to wash my hair, since I'd cut it all off I didn't need much, there was nothing to do in the shower now except stand there and wait to feel reborn, I brought the rough rectangle close to my face to inspect its striations, how much it looked like wet dirt, why had she been digging? I must have stayed in there for an hour, but of course, Berlin, there were still people in my living room when I got out. I kept my face down, even as a voice said my name, and went straight to the bedroom. Theo and Yves lay in my bed, braided together, resting. The room smelled of sperm.

'Hi, darling,' Yves said, lifting an arm towards me.

I went to the window and turned the German-shaped latch, cracking it open. The frozen air streamed in, clean and fast.

'I'm coming in. I need *out* of there,' I said, and burrowed into the blankets, still in my bathrobe with a towel embellishing my head. Yves rubbed my shoulder. 'Mmmm, you smell good,' Theo mewed.

'I hate artists,' I said. They both laughed.

Yves turned to Theo. 'I told you, she's in a heartbreak.'

Theo clicked his tongue. 'Poor you,' he said. From the way he said 'poor,' with the long *o* like a *u* sound, I suddenly recognised that he was German.

'Oh, you're from here?' I said.

He confirmed this by lowering his eyelids and face like someone in prayer.

'The only one who's original.'

That night I dreamt vividly – the kind of dream that feels real while it happens, and upon waking, leaves a residue that convinces you that it did happen – of Hanne. It was the end of the world; we knew this because we had been called upon to save it; we were spies, or some kind of people who had power that was kept secret from the public; we took orders from a nameless, faceless council of men with more power than us; there was an intricate ruse planned by our bosses, to ensnare spies from the other side; it involved luring them to a sex show; Hanne is naked, tied to a large stone, face down, chest flattened, her ass raised; her ankles are chained to the rock by what look like railroad spikes attached to shackles; she has three holes, horizontally puncturing her, all the same size, foaming with pastel-coloured yeast; they look like bullet holes; I am penetrating them, each in turn, methodically going from one to the other after three pumps each; I look down at my long cock; I notice a silver watch on my wrist; I realise that I am Jonah; I panic, I hope no one notices; Hanne starts talking to me, at an intimate volume, saying something about how this is part of the plan; but I can't understand what she's saying, as though she is speaking a foreign language; she starts pointing with her handcuffed hand; I look; the washing-machine-sized earthenware pot of dirt is within arm's reach; as soon as I see this, I understand her; I take the spade and drop dirt on her; it makes a hard, sad sound that feels disrespectful; there is a racket of applause; I'm still pumping with my cock; I look up to see that we are in an amphitheatre, sur-rounded by an audience; I can't make out their faces; at the back, I think I see the scar-woman, turned around, showing me her hole. My phone receives a text message: the sound cuts off the dream and my eyes flap open. It's light out. Theo and Yves are turned away in the bed, curved into spoons, still asleep. I bring the phone to my face, 10 a.m., one new message. My tongue tastes like salt. I open the message, it's from Hanne.

'Did I just pass you on the street?' it says. It's 1 in the morning where she is.

I inhale through my dry mouth and write back 'maybe', then throw the phone to the floor, where its clatter wakes everyone.

I liked the second gallerist I met with, a woman in her mid-50s named Silke, and signed on with her. She wore leather pants to our meeting and had a white streak in her black hair, both of which I took as good omens. Her face was sturdy and square, and a delicate moustache lined her upper lip. She said she was distantly related to Diaghilev, through his stepmother, which Theo later told me couldn't possibly be true, but we decided to believe her anyway, for the sake of the story. My first show with her was to be in the summer, June or July, and, hearing the names of these months – we said them together, first her, 'June or July,' then me, nodding, 'June or July' – flooded my head with bright colours, peach, salmon red, orange, and I immediately said, before thinking, 'There must be pineapple juice served at the opening, and vases of nasturtiums,' to which she let out an accidental giggle and maternally touched my knee. We invited her to Yves's birthday party. On my way home from the meeting, I saw a batch of sparrows stipple the branch of a bald tree; another good omen, I thought.

My infection worsened, so I had to go to the pharmacy to buy cream and the pearlescent, ovoid tablets to insert. The pharmacist was a young man, probably my age, and I watched him shrink under my stare as I told him my symptoms. 'Oh, and, um, Miss,' he said as I took the bag to leave, 'It's – it's – um – it's advisable not to have intercourse penetration for several days.' I pushed my stare at him harder. '*Jesus*, man, I *know*.'

Theo and Yves dragged me out nearly every night, to a bar, a club, a party, to which I'd bring a bottle of cranberry juice and spend most of my time smoking by myself, feeling impatient and bored at the same time; I'd watch them frolic with each other, simple, newborn desire, wrap their arms around the shoulders of their friends, sing loudly with outstretched arms the way I'd seen theatre students do in college, and, as the night wore on, start to dance with each other in little shimmies; after a few hours of this, I'd depart, smiling against their drunkenly quivering eyes and operatic pleas that I stay; I'd sink into the luxury of the cab that sped me away, even if it only took me a few blocks; I couldn't walk more than a couple of steps without my cunt catching fire. I'd think of RuPaul saying, 'Your pussy's on fire!' and then the word 'rue'. *Drag Race* was mine and Yves's favourite show, but I was alone to enjoy the pun. In my flat, the medicine's hot slime oozing out of me, I'd spread out on the bed or some-times the floor, and rest my phone on my chest, so if I fell asleep when Hanne texted, I'd feel it in my bones and wake up. She'd texted a couple of times since that first one, nothing much, 'where are you', 'in Berlin', insignificant notes that shouldn't have provoked anything in me, but with each hour that passed, I felt the urge to resist checking my phone lessen, until I checked it all the time, hearing phantom rings from my bag so that I frantically dug it out to find that it showed me nothing other than the fact that more time had passed; I took the phone with me to the bathroom, laid it on the bar next to my ashtray, fondled it in my coat pocket with my gloved hand, switched it to vibrate *and* ring; when she did text, and her name 'Hanne' appeared on the face of the phone, it was as though her own face was looking at me, the grand, lion eyes; but then I'd see that the eyes I was peering into were instead the reflections of my own, small seed-eyes; I'd swipe my thumb and read whatever she'd sent as my whole body twitched, cunt outwards, to heart, hands, throat, head.

Then, about a week later, came: 'I got the photos back', to which I replied, after waiting a few painful minutes, 'Cool, how are they'. A day went by with no response, then came six in succession with no words, only the photos them-selves, and there she was, no more staring at my own reflection, I was staring at her, there she was, in the phone, in the palm of my hand. She sent these while I was at a quiet bar with Yves, Theo, and some of their friends, and the blings and buzzes from my phone happened during a lull in the conversation, so every-one turned to me then, and watched whatever fluttered in my face indicating I'd received something of value, and Yves reached over and snatched the phone out of my stupid hand; I didn't – couldn't – protest, but fell back in my chair as the group pawed at the phone, rectangular blue glowing on their faces as their awe morphed into a numinous hum, and Hanne's face shrank the world around me. I was alone with her, in a room with glowing walls, ceiling, floor, it was sound-less, I kneeled before her, she looked down on me from very high up, her face curving around us both, becoming the stratosphere; the word 'gold' comes from a Proto-Indo-European word that literally means 'to shine', it was all they could do to describe it, this shining stuff, make a word that was what it was; beneath her skin, I saw her body's circuitry, the blood vessels and nervous system and vital organs and skeleton, the muscle of her heart working calmly, keeping its unbroken but mortal time, I could feel the beats, as though they were in my own chest, I put my hand there, felt the gloating of my heart, her face sucked me up, and I was gone; in the bar, I fell over and cracked my head open on the floor, all I saw was a shining light.

Yves and Theo took me to the hospital. I had to have stitches, a diagonal line across my forehead, which would, Yves said, give me a 'fine and charismatic scar'. I'd also had a concussion, they told me, and would feel strange for some days. 'Ha,' I said, which provoked quizzical looks, so I said, 'I'll feel like myself then,' and Yves started quickly speaking his broken German, in an effort, I'm sure, to assure the doctors that I had not meant it, that I was fine. They asked me if I had allergies, was taking medications, any ailments; I told them about my yeast infection, that I often had migraines, no allergies; 'My mother, though, my mother had problems,' I found myself saying, 'my sister and I inherited a family curse!' but it seemed as though no one heard me, or was listening any more, I raised my voice, 'My mother, my mother was fucked up, she was cursed!' then, when they turned to me, again with baffled faces, embarrassment washed over my face, and my throat thickened; I had trouble breathing and a nurse stroked my shoulder; everyone called me 'Miss', which they never did any more in America; there, I was old, I was 'Ma'am'; Yves took me home, without Theo; I'd always appreciated his perceptiveness. When I'd climbed into bed, and he'd patted the blanket up around my neck, he pulled my phone out of his pocket.

'At least now I know why you're a mess,' he said, holding it up. 'Fallen for another white girl, tsk, tsk.'

'Oh fuck, I didn't respond yet!' I lurched up and grabbed for the phone. He waved it out of reach.

'I'll write it, I'll write it. You just rest, sweetheart.'

I waved my arms. The contempt in the word 'sweetheart' caught my fear. 'But what are you going to *say*? It has to be the exact right thing! You have to be perfect!'

'Mmm, I'll just say that seeing these things put you in the hospital.'

'Fuck! Stop it! *Yves*!' My voice was violent and pathetic and I stretched forward with enough force that Yves stood up and backed into the wall.

He said my name in a low voice, not as an address, or a question, but as though to himself, to describe the thing he was looking at. 'I've never seen you like this.' We stared hard at each other for a moment, a minor battle, then he breathed quickly, and said, 'Take your pain pill. I'll come by in the morning.' He left the room, still with my phone, and was out of the flat by the time I'd flung myself out of the bed and flailed into the living room. The blood that rushed to my forehead crashed into the wall behind my eyes, and I pitched forward, hands dropping into the cushions of the sofa. I vomited a bitter, clear liquid, then slunk back to bed. That night, I dreamed of Hanne again, but the medication suffocated my memory of it, and I awoke the next morning as though I'd fallen out of time, but there was the stain on the couch I had to get out.

I spent the next days, in bed, high on pain medication, with Yves dropping by once in the morning and once in the evening with food, and not bringing my phone with him. When I asked, his voice was imperious; he said only, 'I've handled her,' to which I fizzed with anxiety, 'What the *fuck* does that *mean*? *Yves!*' But he didn't respond to these demands, and went on to talk calmly about the preparations for his birthday party, who was coming, who he didn't want to invite but felt obligated to, the food, how there must be flowers. After maybe a week, maybe longer, he said, 'Remember, it's tomorrow night. You'll be well enough by then, I'm sure. Just don't drink too much.' He flattened his hand on top of my thigh, holding it there for a moment, pressing slightly in an effort to repeat his instructions without having to say them again, then got up to leave, but stopped, turned, and told me, 'In the morning, the cleaners are coming. They'll need some time to shampoo the sofa. I'm afraid, my dear, you didn't get all the mess out.'

I wanted to wear something imposing for the party; I needed protection, to be intimidating. While the cleaners worked, and Yves and Theo set up the flat in the late afternoon, I stayed locked in my room, then in the tub, with the water up to my chin, feeling leaden and edgeless. I needed my edges if I were to get through the night, so I dressed in a black lace turtleneck with long sleeves, kept together by a fine transparent gauze underneath, and black leather gloves that went nearly to my elbows, elongating my fingers into claws. The spidery lace clung to my breasts like a web, and I wore no bra, so that people would have to fight with themselves when talking to me, use their will power to keep their gaze on my face, this could be a game I'd amuse myself with; and I lengthened myself with tight, high-waisted black pants and the over-the-knee, black leather stiletto boots that I only wore when I was depressed and needed to feel big. I removed the bandage from my forehead, so the black stitches stuck out in delicate spikes, there were still a few dots of dried blood around the red slit, and I drew black lines around my eyes the way Zinat used to do. When I emerged, Yves and Theo cooed and fanned their faces.

Many people came, most of whom I knew, friends of Yves's who I'd become friends with over the years, our many parties, other people I'd been in rooms with before but didn't know beyond polite acknowledgements, and then the ones Yves had felt obligated to invite, curators and big names who I made a point of avoiding; Yves sauntered around in a perfect suit the colour of ivory; I saw a small group of dancer-looking young people, nimble limbs twisting together with each other and the furniture, who had to be Theo's friends; there were

a few old flings of mine, we exchanged reserved nods; Silke appeared, as promised, with her husband, who was quite short and much older than her, with
a spherical bald head and red face, and we chatted affably, but I don't remember
what about, though I felt pleased with myself for choosing her, and left them
feeling victorious; the pain medication and alcohol wrapped me in a heavy film
of numb warmth; everyone looked beautiful; Yves and Theo had done a lovely
job getting the flat ready; there were elaborate flowers everywhere, how did they
manage that when the most you can buy in German wintertime are hothouse
carnations? I went into the kitchen, to refill my glass, and found a small group
huddled around the table, being told a story by someone I didn't see. A smooth,
masculine voice flowed out from the centre of the group. He kept his voice at
a volume like he was speaking into one person's ear, his mouth close enough to
their head that his breath fell on the innocent skin of their neck. The air was
poised and sincere, all the attention on him; no one noticed me, so I faced the
sink, my back to them, and listened.

'I'd just moved out of the house with my soulmate – or who I *thought* had
been my soulmate – and back into the tiny, rat-infested cabin where I'd lived
before I met her. There was rat shit on all the books I'd left behind, and in the
corners of all the windows, there were fat spiders sucking the guts out of, like,
really fat flies. There were no mangoes or oranges, like she'd always kept around,
or, for that matter, warm water or heat. I was reading – ah, what was it – I think
Infinite Jest – by a *torch lantern*, of all things, that, of course, attracted mosquitoes.
And I had to wear socks all the time to keep off the ticks.'

'Wait, I'm sorry,' someone interrupted him. '*Where* was this again?'

'In L. A. – well, Altadena, it's called. It's sort of in the hills behind L. A.'

My thoughts wrinkled: I had grown up in Altadena.

'The cabin,' the voice kept going, smoothing me out, 'was near a little creek
that was mostly dry, but it had just rained – this was in the winter, the only time
it rains in L. A. – so it was muddy and there was some water in it. We were on a
pretty steep hill, with trees all around. Anyway, my roommate worked nights,
and he had this really old dog. She had been a great dog: smart, calm, the perfect
size, like, kind of like, ottoman-sized' – people laughed – 'and she was the same
colour as a female lion, you know, beautiful and tawny, with those gold eyes.
Her name was Ava, and she really was special. But she was *really* old at that
point, I mean, totally deaf, blind, had trouble walking, and had these disgusting little tumours, like, *bulging* out of her fur, with, like, a *crust* on them – you
know, an *old* dog. She spent all day lying on this nasty cushion in the living
room, just, like, panting. Her ribs had started to show through. I kept asking
my roommate what he was gonna do with her, but he just couldn't, you know,
just couldn't put her down. She was like his wife. That's what he'd say. "You
can't kill your own wife!" So, anyway, there I am, reading fucking *Infinite Jest*
by fucking candlelight, to keep from crying about my dumb pain, it's almost
midnight, the frogs in the creek are croaking this, like, seamless buzz, like' – he

stopped to hum – 'and then comes this tiny cry of an animal. It sounded like a thought in the back of my own head. Just: blinked in, and then out. I couldn't be sure if it was the frogs or my own head, you know? But then it came again. I sat up. Again. This hollow, small *yip*' – he made his voice squeak – 'I called for her, Ava, even though she couldn't hear me, I mean, of course, there was no answer. So I pulled out some pants and a sweatshirt from, like, a paper bag – nothing was unpacked yet – and stumbled out the back, down towards the creek. I remembered that my roommate had said she'd gotten stuck down there before. So I'm out there, in the dark, and I just, I just' – he paused, probably making a hand gesture that I couldn't see – '*hated everything* – the entire world, everyone in it, God, or whoever the fuck – hated it *all*. And I'm calling her name, and it's just going from my mouth into the trees. There's only the frogs, the mud, the night, and me. I started to cry out, 'Talk to me! Tell me where you are!' To a deaf, blind dog in the dark. Like, at the end of the earth in the pit of night. Can you imagine? *Talk to me, talk to me*? Like I was saying it to God! Like, I'm one of those people trying to get God to listen to them!' It made me smile, almost snicker, but everyone was quiet. I heard him lick his lips. 'And then, I fell into a fucking patch of poison oak, and then into some mud near the creek, and one of my knees hit me in the throat, so I'm just, like, so *fucking* miserable – hitting myself in the throat with my *own* knee? – Jesus! – you know? – but then' – he paused – 'I saw her. The cataracts in her eyes caught my flashlight. They were these glowing milky orbs in the dark. I could make her out, down the hill, her tiny body. It was the size of a toddler. She was all crumpled between some rocks. I scrambled down to her and just blurted out, 'I've got you, baby,' but, but, like, I don't know, when I said it, it felt like a lie. Like, what am I saying? What if I can't save her? What then? I reached between the rocks, and scraped my hands to shit, trying to pull her out. She was so terrified – I could feel her heart beating against her ribs, like a bird was trapped in there – I mean, she's blind *and* deaf, *total darkness* – and all she knows is that she's trapped in between some hard things and in pain and probably getting ready to fucking die, just give it, like, the fuck up, you know? So, she's squirming and I pull harder and she makes her little noise again, and then – I don't know – I got her free. We both fell over, but I got her out. Her body went limp, like, with total trust in me. I carried her up the hill, and then we just collapsed, both of us, on her smelly, disgusting, crusty cushion in the living room. Her front paws were all bloody, and my hands were all scratched up and bleeding, and we were both covered in mud. My wet pants turned warm under her body, like I'd peed in them, or maybe she'd peed on me, I don't know. I wrapped her in a towel, and we sat there together, both shaking, for I don't know how long. When I woke up the next morning, and went in to check on her, she was still alive, and – and, I don't know – I don't how to describe it to you – but – it felt – like a miracle.'

There was a clap, like a hand had been slapped definitively on the table, and the people around the voice collectively exhaled. I could hear the creaking of their chairs as they fell back in them, then a throat loudly gulped wine, probably the throat that'd housed that voice. I turned around, in a trance, the voice crawling through me, and found my eyes on Jonah. Everyone else was staring at him too. My high pooled in my head and I felt a rustle in my body. A woman, an older woman I didn't recognise, wrapped in a silky shawl, reached her hand out and laid it on top of his. In a thick accent that sounded Slavic, she said, 'You are a saint,' to which everyone clapped, laughed, grinned, nodded. To the cheering, Jonah kissed the woman's hand, then stood up, raised his arm, and bowed deeply, so that his hair brushed her lap, his nose in her crotch. There was more clapping and a few cheers. When he returned to being upright, he turned his head and spotted me. His eyes dropped immediately to my breasts, then snapped back to my face, and something scattered his expression, both graceless and discerning; he turned and addressed the group abruptly, 'I think I need a cigarette now, you'll have to excuse me,' then he grazed me again with his eyes, and, hooked, I followed him to the balcony.

The cold outside cut through my spider web, and I sharpened on the outside but loosened on the inside. Jonah looked for a while, flagrantly, but with appreciation, one side of his mouth slyly pulled up, as though I were a work of art he'd just purchased, and he lit his cigarette, stared a few moments more, then drew his eyes up from my tits, cocked his head, and said, 'So.' His voice was still at the level it had been during the story, like his mouth was very close. My limbs tingled, I'd drunk too much. 'What happened to your head?' he said, and then he was stroking my face, lifting strands of hair away from the wound, I could smell his mouth, its stench of cigarette and wine, and then his chest pressed into mine, my nipples like needles, pinching me more than him. 'Have you seen your dirt-woman again? Your cave-woman, you cave-woman?' His voice felt kind and magical. What? 'What?' I was startled to hear my own voice sound so far away, like my mouth was speaking from across the courtyard. I wanted to rest my face in his palm. My head felt weighted down. I bent it forward. His hand was soft, warm, and dry as it cupped my chin. He gently turned my head side to side and asked me things, I don't remember what exactly, but I felt a tender fog envelop me, and his soft coat was around my shoulders, and then we were in a cab, sailing through the city as the lights streaked into lines of gold and his sibilant voice breathed into my ear, falling on my innocent neck.

As we stood outside his building's door and he fished for his keys, I saw there was a great moon above us. I tried to point it out, but now the door was open, and he was pulling me inside, so I left it out there, the ball of light, like a present I'd brought but forgot to give him. He put a pot on the stove and brewed a fantastic tea that had whole flower heads in it. The cashmere scarf had been unwound from his neck, although I couldn't be sure if he'd been wearing it tonight, if I'd only remembered it from the other night, and I saw that he had an exquisitely thin, breakable little neck, like a girl's. For the first time, I noticed that he had oily black hair and sea-green eyes, like me. Jonah. What was his real name again?

'I miss the mourning doves.' His voice was wreathed in the steam from the tea. 'Pale, grief-stricken pigeons. I grew up with them. They're everywhere in L. A. In New York, too. They mate for life. Their wings whistle when they fly. That sound is what summer sounds like to me. But they don't have them here. Not even in the summer. I asked.'

'But there are so many of those cute tiny ones, that chatter all the time, looking for stuff to eat. They're like little black lumps in the bare branches.'

He seemed not to have heard me. I wondered if we'd been speaking out loud.

'We have the same shoes!' one of us said, but that couldn't have been true.

'You look like someone from one of my paintings,' I said. Again, he made no sign that I'd spoken.

I tasted like candy, he said after he'd kissed me, and then there was a plate of fluffy pink cake in front of me. The boiled flowers in my tea had opened themselves and become sodden and pulpy, lurid purples and reds, like the inner organs of an animal; I saw my mother's dresses in their steaming baths of dye, as she leaned over them, stirring with a long wooden spoon. A vision came into my head of her shit on the floor, the bodies of dead fish, sodden, clotted, but also rounded and soft, confections made of coloured sugar and twinkling, moist mousse. When his bare shoulders touched the insides of my thighs, I felt that my skin was clammy and it reminded me of who I was, making me tractable as he spread me apart. He used his middle finger in time with his tongue; someone gracious had taught him that, I thought; and my head skimmed along with the flicks and waves, then fell away.

'Um,' his face was in front of mine, yanking me out of my swim. 'Um, I think you – you have an infection.' He touched his tongue against the roof of his mouth, forming an oval, tasting the poison in it.

My hands shot down to cover myself. 'I'm sorry,' I said.

He lifted his face coyly. 'You're what now?'

'I'm,' I felt alone, 'I'm sorry, Jonah. Sorry.'

'Oh,' he clucked his tongue, 'but I can't hear you. *What* are you?'

Something brutal flitted across his eyes. I understood the game, but couldn't remember if I'd wanted to play.

He pulled my wrists off of myself and pressed them into the bed, like Jesus. 'You're sorry?' with a simpering command at the end, 'hm?' I heard the cruelty behind his soft voice starting to lurch up, and my voice was pure when I sang, like a lullaby, 'I'm sorry I'm sorry Jonah Jonah Jonah.' Then, his fingers were in my mouth, pressing down the rows of my bottom teeth, opening my mouth too far, I heard my jaw crack as he stretched it open. They were pillowy, his fingers, like the pads of a dog's feet. His thumb braced the underside of my chin. 'I want you to sing for me,' his voice was majestic in its roughness, 'come on and sing for me.' He laughed at the dismal, lapping sounds that came out of my spread mouth.

I was naked, on my hands and knees, and he wore a suit, with a black jacket and pants, his cock rising out of the opened fly. Had he always been wearing that? 'Keep singing, dove,' he said, as he hooked two fingers into the flesh of my face, like the bit of a bridle. My mouth was pricked by my medicine. He started to ride me from behind, not quickly, but hard and punishing, a blow with each word, I felt it deep in my belly, my liver, thud, thud, thud. 'Come on, now. Coo for me. Coo, like a bird.' The sounds coming out of me deepened into guttural moans, and at these, he slapped me, my ass, my face, 'don't be like that, dove,' the slaps stung with reward, 'keep singing, be pretty for me,' then he rolled me over, 'don't you want to be my pretty slut?' I swallowed the words, nodded yes, yes, yes, the sick relief in yielding, he pressed his hand into my face, my head pushed deep and sideways into the pillows, I felt swaddled, small, safe in my smallness, there was the crushing smell of my anti-fungal cream, and my cunt's bread, and the salt of his hand, through the fingers I watched his sallow chest rocking over me, he pumped like he was trying to unclog a drain, 'now, say my name,' slapped my face, 'say it', slap, 'say it', *Jonah*, I muttered into the down, two lost syllables that filled my mouth, brain, body, *slap*, again but harder now, vicious, *slap*, 'that's not my fucking name, bitch,' slap, slap, *slap*, then the hand was around my neck, pulling me up from the bed, close to his face so I saw his eyes drenched with scorn, alive with it, I'd never seen anyone so happy, and the hand tightened its grip, so I couldn't speak his name even if I had known it; my world shrank to a pinpoint of his eye, black like a jewel; my face filled with heat, and then there was a lot of wetness on it, wetness everywhere, it dripped down my neck; I saw the eye widen with thrill; I reached up to touch my forehead, my hand hopping because of his thrusts, and when I felt my stitches covered in slime, and pulled my hand away and saw it glazed with red, I tried to scream, opening my mouth in a vain, soundless O; nothing but a bronchial whistle seeped out, and seeing this small struggle of mine got him to his end. He rolled off and fell asleep, in his suit jacket and pants, cock withered and harmless. I lie there, without moving, trying not to think of the damage, for a long time. Then, a little strength came to pull myself up, dab the blood with some white clothing of his I found on the floor, I wanted to leave him some stains, and I got dressed in my ineffective spiderweb. When I looked over at him, on my way out, I saw that in sleep, he looked innocent, thoughtless, like a child – it felt insulting, I could've killed him by pushing my thumb through his fontanelle.

On my way out, I saw a small object on a bookcase, I recognised it, I'd seen it before, it was the height of a coffee mug, a lumpy piece of bronze in the crude shape of a dog, the paws very large as though a child had drawn them, the head and muzzle clumsily formed in wads; now I remembered, it was a replica of a large sculpture by a famous artist, I couldn't think of the artist's name, I remembered we had to study it in school; I picked it up; very heavy, heavier than I thought; turned it over; a number and signature were scratched into the bottom; an official edition or something, must be worth a lot; it was heavy enough to club someone to death despite being small enough to sit in my hand; I felt its weight in my palm as a kind of dim, ersatz power as I walked out into the street. The sky was getting light.

BALKAN ODYSSEY
ALEV SCOTT

ESSAY

On a 500-year-old humpbacked bridge in Mostar, southern Bosnia, a sunburnt man in tiny swimming trunks is collecting coins from tourists. After ten minutes, he hands the money to a friend before stepping onto the crest of the bridge. Breathing deeply and stretching like an Olympic champion, he pauses for a moment before simply stepping off and plunging feet-first into the green water 24 metres below. Robbed of a proper diving performance, the crowd nevertheless bursts into nervous applause as he surfaces from the water, alive.

Spanning the River Neretva near the modern-day border with Croatia, the Stari Most bridge was commissioned by the Ottoman sultan, Suleyman the Magnificent, in 1566. Impressive even today, it was at its completion the widest man-made arch in the world; the seventeenth-century travel writer Evliya Çelebi described it as 'like heaven's rainbow... a bridge so high it seems to be connecting two clouds'. Walking gingerly over the slippery cobbles in flip-flops, I remember the local story that the original bridge was held together by egg-white mortar, an unglamorous but apparently effective technique that lasted 427 years – even as heavy artillery thundered across during the Second World War – until the bridge was targeted and destroyed by Croat shells in 1992 during the Bosnian war. In 2004, UNESCO began careful reconstruction with the original stones, and now the bridge stands as though untouched while the town itself is riddled with bullet holes and craters. On many of the half-smashed Brutalist buildings, '1981' is scrawled in red graffiti paint – the year the local Velež football club, which united the town's Croats, Serbs and Bosniaks in fierce support, won the Yugoslav cup, before one of the most horrifically violent wars of the twentieth century.

The Yugoslavian history of Mostar has now been eclipsed by its more picturesque Ottoman history as tourists flock to see the reconstructed bridge. In the centre of town, the twisted alleyways are packed with souvenir stands under the eaves of striped black-and-white Ottoman houses that look quasi-Tudor to an English eye. Most of the tourists wandering around are mildly adventurous, middle-aged Turks bussed in from Sarajevo in the north. After their excursions, they sit in restaurants by the river, happily eating kebabs and marvelling at the legacy of their ancestors. 'Isn't it all amazing?' they gush. I was to witness a lot of this nostalgic tourism at play in the Balkans, a strange tour of inspection of former territories by today's Turks; a collective basking in reflected historical glory.

After Suleyman's conquests of the sixteenth century, the Ottomans controlled a vast swathe of European land, stretching from Istanbul to the gates of Vienna and encompassing the Balkans, Greece and even Odessa in southern Ukraine. From the fourteenth century, the Balkans made up the longstanding core of the Ottomans' western territories, lasting until the early twentieth century when the emergence of the concept of a nation state inspired rebellion among people who were suddenly made aware of their 'Bosnian' or 'Bulgarian' identities. Sultan Mehmet V fought to keep these territories in the First Balkan War of 1912 and lost: the beginning of the end of the Empire – in its old incarnation, at least.

Today, mosques, bridges, caravanserais and *hamams* in various states of disrepair reflect the Ottoman glory period, which emerged after the sixteenth-century conquests of land stretching from the gates of Vienna to Odessa. The bridges have survived best; the Stari Most is one of the most famous of these, but is surpassed by the Mehmed Paša Sokolović Bridge in Višegrad, the subject of the 1943 novel *Bridge On The Drina* by Bosnian Nobel Laureate Ivo Andrić. Most of the mosques of the region were destroyed either by Communist authorities in the mid-twentieth century or, more comprehensively, in the Balkan Wars between 1992 and 1995, but Turkey has come to the rescue, flexing its regional muscles after barely a century's rest.

As I travelled around the Balkans, I was looking for the legacy of the Ottoman Empire in all its forms – architectural, political and social – and found it in unexpected places: the whirling dervish lodges of Sarajevo, the separatists of southern Serbia, villages of Turkish-speaking car mechanics in the Kosovan countryside and the tea gardens of Skopje's old bazaar. I also found a Turkish zone of influence overlying the region, one largely created by money, but also by the strategic reinvigoration of latent loyalty to an old empirical power.

In the past decade or so of Erdoğan's rule, the Turkish government has been busy rebuilding Ottoman-era mosques, bridges and *hamams* with millions of euros of taxpayers' money, as well as brand new mosques, universities and cultural institutes. A few hundred yards from the Stari Most bridge in Mostar is a perfectly restored sixteenth-century *hamam*, oddly sterile, and in Skopje, the capital of Macedonia, the entrance hall of the fifteenth-century Çifte Hamamı has been transformed into a gallery, light twinkling down through the domed roof onto contemporary art exhibits. Imagine the Italian government suddenly pouring money into restoring previously neglected Roman ruins across Europe, with a view to promoting Italy's empirical past and, by extension, its current standing in the world. The Turkish-Ottoman equivalent seemed absurd and vainglorious as I encountered it at the start of my journey; as I headed south, it made more sense.

In the aftermath of the USSR, the decline of the European Union and the rise of religious tensions, the Balkan states are trying to define themselves in the twenty-first century, stuck awkwardly on the edge of Europe. Turkey is by no means the only interested bidder for influence in the region. Driving across Bosnia, Serbia, Kosovo, Macedonia and Bulgaria, I noticed half-empty buildings everywhere, and this construction boom seemed to mirror the semi-constructed, aspirational state of the countries themselves. The region is ripe for more powerful states to carve out influence; Russia and Turkey are currently gaining on the ebbing influence of the EU and NATO in the former Yugoslavia and its surrounding region.

Bosnia is a study in modern imperialism; while 500 years ago the country was occupied by Ottoman forces, it is now occupied by Turkish money. I visited Mostar on a swelteringly hot day last July, and after watching the sunburnt faux-diver performing for tourists, I passed over to the east bank of the Neretva, where a magnificent, red-and-white-striped building flies a large, red-and-white Turkish flag; this is the local Yunus Emre Institute, a governmental organisation set up a decade ago by then-Prime Minister Erdoğan as a kind of worldwide cultural franchise. The single staff member on duty in the Mostar branch – a burly man who spoke Turkish with a strong Bosnian accent – looked astonished to see me. The building was totally empty, the walls plastered with Turkish language charts ('B for Baklava', etc), pristine classrooms awaiting phantom hordes of eager Bosnian students. Despite boasting only twelve Turks, Mostar also maintains a Turkish embassy well-stocked with leaflets about Istanbul's finest museums, and genuine Turkish staff, full of the zeal of missionaries.

Much more so than Mostar, Sarajevo is a Little Turkey. Bosnia's capital was founded by the Ottomans in 1461 and is a beautiful, tragic city of cemeteries, surrounded by hills occupied by Serbian paramilitaries less than thirty years ago, and still haunted by trauma. Today every slope within the city hosts a swathe of white tombstones, many of them the graves of those killed in the recent war, others clearly Ottoman, with the recognisable turban-like headstone of the Sufi Bektashi order. Signs of the war are everywhere: the recently restored town hall was once a library, shelled by Serbian forces in 1992. In the fire that resulted, the one and a half million books, many of them Ottoman, were burned – in the underground archive space, only black-and-white photographs of the collection remain. On the floors and walls of the building itself, almost too perfectly restored, the replicated Jewish star of David and Islamic-style calligraphic art reflect the multi-layered history of the city, visible today because of punctilious archaeologists paid by the EU.

On the streets of the old city of Sarajevo, all I could hear was the Turkish spoken by tourists flown in from Istanbul by the national carrier airline, heavily subsidised by the government. The red-and-white crescent and star is ubiquitous, flying from half-restored monuments and souvenir shops, touting for custom by claiming an imperial past. On the top of a hill above the old city juts a fifteenth-century whirling dervish lodge, destroyed by Communist authorities in 1956 and rebuilt by the Turkish municipality of Konya, an uber-conservative town in central Anatolia, in 2013. Trudging up through a cemetery to reach it, I found a spotless, Alpine chalet-like building perched on a tiny, flower-filled outcrop of land. It was utterly empty and in immaculate condition, like the Yunus Emre Institute in Mostar. Inside, I found bookshelves filled with Turkish editions of the Koran and a silent caretaker who offered me tea. Outside were neat flowerbeds and a brass plaque proudly informing visitors that in 2013, then-Foreign Minister Ahmet Davutoglu (a bespectacled chipmunk of a professor-turned-politician, and the architect of Turkey's current nouveau-Ottoman foreign policy), opened this lodge on behalf of the Republic of Turkey. Near the airport is the International University of Sarajevo, founded in 2004 by a group of businessmen close to then-Prime Minister Erdoğan (who himself opened the new campus in 2010) with 65 per cent Turkish students. When I visited, a large poster hung on the side of the main building celebrating the upcoming anniversary of the defeated 2016 coup in Turkey, in keeping with the fierce promotion of the anniversary by the Turkish government.

The eastern region of Bosnia, near the border with Serbia, is where Turkish influence begins to give way to Russian, where more recent Soviet control trumps Ottoman legacy. Churches replace mosques in the villages along the way, and within an hour of Sarajevo you come to a battleground of historical narrative and a monument to artistic vanity in the form of the Bosnian town of Višegrad, just 10 kilometres from the border.

Here, Emir Kusturica, the film director as famous for his surreal, Palme d'Or-winning art as for his political views, has built a fake village within the town. In early 2011, he announced he would be making a film adaptation of *Bridge On the Drina*, and the resulting film set, Andrićgrad, is mired in controversy. Kusturica, born in Sarajevo, is widely despised by his fellow Bosnians for, they say, renouncing his heritage and embracing both the Serbian government and its attendant Russian patronage (he converted to the Serbian Orthodox Church on St George's Day, 2005, and received the Order of Friendship from President Putin eleven years later). Like the French actor Gerard Depardieu, Russian friendship has cost him dear.

Andrićgrad is as much a political statement as a cultural project. It is first and foremost an homage to Andrić, the novelist who wrote *Bridge On The Drina*, a story which features Ottoman tyranny in the sixteenth century, in particular the heartbreak that went into building the bridge and the cruelties perpetrated on the Christian locals forced into slave labour by Ottoman overlords. Today, the bridge serves as a symbol of tension between Muslims and Christians, and this tension is intertwined with nationalist politics. In 1992, Serbian paramilitaries massacred thousands of Bosniak men, women and children in the Višegrad region. Many of them were shot and then thrown from the bridge, and Bosniak women were systematically raped in nearby hotels. The bridge became a symbol of the retribution of Christians against Muslims, supposedly righting the wrongs perpetrated against their Ottoman subject forefathers hundreds of years ago. In a horrible way, Andrić's book inspired these reciprocal twentieth-century massacres, and Kusturica's film project is a strange seal of approval in the guise of Art.

The approach to Višegrad is utterly dominated by the magnificent Mehmed Pasa Sokolovic Bridge, its multiple arches stretching for 180 metres from bank to bank of the Drina. Unlike the Stari Most, the bridge survived the 1992 war unscathed and stands in its original glory today. As I walked over it, an elderly fisherman stood in his wellies in the shallows below, a peaceful scene utterly at odds with the bridge's bloody history. On the western bank, I turned left and walked on to the gates of Andrićgrad, which may one day serve as a film set, but currently operates as far as I could see purely a tourist attraction, complete with a large cinema (showing *The Emoji Movie* and *Planet of the Apes* at the time of my visit), a prominent (empty) church jutting out spectacularly into the Drina, replica Ottoman houses functioning as cafes, and a large central statue of Andrić. Serbian tourists throng its streets and large murals of Putin and other Communist leaders grace the walls of the cafes, alongside modern Serbian heroes like Novak Djokovic. Outside an obscure 'science centre' is a statue of Serbian-born Nikola Tesla.

There is no mention anywhere of the 1992 massacres; it is one of the most astonishing disavowals of history I have ever seen. The town of Višegrad itself, largely devoid of Muslims after the massacres, is equally bereft of signs of the conflict – the most famous of the 'rape hotels', where Serbian soldiers systematically raped local Bosniak women, is the Vilina Vlas, now a spa with glowing online reviews ('four stars – great place to relax').

I tracked down Kusturica just over the Serbian border in his other film-set village, Drvengrad, originally built for his film *Life Is A Miracle* and since used as a venue for cultural festivals. At the time of my visit in July, it was hosting the Bolshoi Music Festival, sponsored by the giant energy company Gazprom, which is majority-owned by the Russian state and a by-word for Russian power in the region. As I approached the village, a helicopter circled overhead; by the time I had parked, an excited crowd had gathered near a helipad, among them two young Chinese women who had travelled all the way from Beijing for a glimpse of their idol. 'He's here! He's here!' Another fan turned to us, her face shining with the euphoria of proximity to Greatness. 'Did you see what he was carrying? A watermelon!' Opinion was divided about the symbolic or pragmatic role of Kusturica's watermelon, recently purchased in Belgrade.

Wandering around the fake village were journalists from *Russia Today* carrying cameras; the crowd seemed composed mainly of Russian press, the musicians themselves, and a few evangelical Kusturica fans like the

Chinese women. I was handed a press card and told to stand by for my interview, but first there was a concert to attend: a 10-year-old girl in a puffy white dress, her feet barely touching the pedals, played Scott Joplin on a Steinway piano with great vivacity. The general effect of the fake film-set village, the high altitude, strong Serbian wine and child prodigy made me feel slightly dizzy. In the interval, I was beckoned for my moment with the *maestro*. He stood in commanding fashion on stage as minions milled around him, a Soviet Quentin Tarantino, powerfully built in his shabby suit, with a shock of unruly grey hair. As his PR assistant announced my credentials, he scowled.

'Why should I give you an interview?' he demanded. 'The fucking British press always make me look like a bastard – the *Spectator* called me a child-murderer.'

I had no answer to this, so I opted for compliance. 'Mr Kusturica – what would you like to tell the British people?'

Momentarily disconcerted, he launched into a glowing account of the success of his cultural festivals. I asked him about the legacy of war in the region in which he chooses to base himself and his projects.

'I turn war zones into cultural events', he declared. 'This is territory which we can say is no man's land – as it was during World War One and World War Two. It is a borderline.'

It soon became apparent that Kusturica thinks of himself as the Andrić of his time, transforming the legacy of war into art, and the legacy of art into a kind of hybrid homage both to himself and his idol, Andrić.

'Since the Drina has such a bloody past, Andrić devoted himself to art. Therefore, I wanted to devote a town to Andrić.'

But can you make a cultural space that does not acknowledge the past, or rather, which selectively acknowledges the past, as in the case of Andrićgrad?

Kusturica frowned. 'We can't forget the past. No – actually, we can. We have atrocities committed on both sides. We have the Srebenica story, which is also terrible. The oil fields in the Middle East are also war zones. The list goes on.'

Kusturica is well-known for his belief that the West is hypocritical in its criticism of Yugoslavian history. His whataboutery had a note of finality, so I turned to the issue of his reputation among Bosnians. While Kusturica is courted in international circles and lauded at Cannes, his countrymen reject him. How does that feel – does he feel any infinity with Orhan Pamuk, the Turkish Nobel Laureate, who is hated by many Turks for publicly acknowledging the Armenian Genocide of 1915, and who needs a bodyguard while on Turkish soil?

'Yes, I feel a great artistic affinity.' But what about a political affinity?

'Oh, you mean the threats against my life? I don't care about them. I write, I play music, I get on with my life. I see the purpose of life as doing my art and creating cultural events.'

As I noted this down, Kusturica reconsidered.

'Actually, many Bosnians love me. You could stop a man in Goražde [in a region of eastern Bosnia with a majority Christian, pro-Serbian population, like Višegrad] and he would worship me. You don't under-stand, it's not just the elite who know about me.'

I noted this also, dutifully. Then I asked him what he wants to be remembered for.

'I saved three goals when I was eight years old, for Sarajevo Football Club. That was my transcendence to immortality. The Palme d'Or – that is nothing'. He gestured dismissively. The interview was over.

From Drvengrad I headed Russia-wards, north to Belgrade. On the way, I noticed the minarets peter out entirely; instead, church spires and cemeteries filled with crosses dotted the countryside. Bosnia and Serbia are striking in their confluence of ethnicity and religion; relatively few Bosnians are Christian, and relatively few Serbians are Muslim, hence the bitterness of the recent conflict. This ethno-religious divide is reflected in countries' geopolitical alliances: while Bosnia welcomes Turkey and its money, Russia is a longstanding 'big brother' to Serbia, and Putin's popularity is high among ordinary Serbians. Most Serbians I spoke to seemed to see no paradox in wanting to be part of Europe while harbouring a vaguer but more visceral attachment to the old Soviet Union. Part of this is undoubtedly down to religious affiliation, however mute this is. Even the most secular of both Serbians and Bosnians seem attuned to being *not* Muslim or Christian, respectively – not 'the other' – and both Turkey and Russia exploit this faultline.

The road into Belgrade betrays Serbia's reliance on Russian and Chinese money – Samsung and Huawei-emblazoned skyscrapers greet visitors coming into the city, and a new bridge – the 'Chinese Bridge'— has been built over the Danube by the Chinese, in exchange for a massive loan to the Serbian government. Belgrade was once a frontier of the Ottoman Empire; in 1521, seventy years after an initial siege, Suleyman the Magnificent succeeded in conquering the Byzantine fort which still dominates the southern side of the city, in the centre of Kalemegdan Park (*kale* from Turkish 'castle' and *megdan*, 'battlefield'). The Christian inhabitants were carted off to the outskirts of Istanbul, to an area which became known as the Belgrade Forest, where rich Turks today play golf and relax in gated villas far from the political smog of the city. The visible Ottoman legacy of Belgrade today is patchy, confined mainly to ruins rather than urban architecture; Zemun, a northern suburb twenty minutes' drive away, was only briefly occupied by the Ottomanss and was indeed a separate village until 1934. You can tell – it is unmistakably and recently Austro-Hungarian, full of picturesque churches and pastel-coloured, European-looking houses.

Walking around the ramparts of the Belgrade fortress, I was reminded of Topkapi Palace in Istanbul, dominating the once-forested peninsula on the southern European side of Istanbul. Today, Turkish tourists wandering around Kalemegdan Park are looking primarily for Ottoman ruins, such as the fountain erected in honour of Mehmed Pasa Sokolovic, of Višegrad fame, or the old Amam (*hamam*), erected in the seventeenth century below the steep ramparts of the fort. I tagged along with one Turkish tour group who grumbled when they discovered the mausoleum of an Ottoman pasha obscured by scaffolding – not quite the gratifying sight of colonial glory they came for.

Despite wielding far less influence in Serbia than in Muslim-majority Balkan countries such as Bosnia, the emissaries of Turkish soft power are hard at work here too, like travelling sales reps pounding the streets of unlikely but possible customers. In Kalmegdan Park, a large photography exhibition honoured the defeat of the 2016 coup attempt. Looking closely at the blown-up photographs of angry citizens attacking tanks and President Erdoğan attending the funerals of the slain, I noticed the sponsor of the exhibition: TIKA, a Turkish government directorate explicitly devoted to funding projects in Turkic or Turkish-speaking communities, founded in 1991 after the fall of the USSR. Its website states that 'Turkey and the countries in Central Asia consider themselves as one nation containing different countries.' In the early

2000s, TIKA expanded into the Balkans, and then Africa and even Latin America, pushing beyond its original remit of Turkic or Turkish-related communities to pastures ever more ambitious.

The Kalemegdan photo exhibition, which was produced by Anadolu Ajansı, one of Turkey's semi-state news outlets, also popped up like a travelling propaganda installation further south in my Balkan travels, for example in the Muslim town of Novi Pazar, centre of the southern Serbia area of Sandžak. The town itself feels conservative – many women wear headscarves, and only one bar openly serves alcohol – but the gambling shops on the high street proclaim Serbia's liberal laws.

Turkish influence is particularly strong near the Serbian-Kosovan border; the Sandžak region was an important administrative area of the Ottoman Empire. The usual Turkish-funded mosques are here, along with branches of Turkish banks (including the state Halk Bank), and the Istanbul-based organisation 'Friends of Sandžak' facilitates marriages, language classes and general support networks between the Serbians who emigrated in large numbers to Turkey over the past twenty years, and Serbia-based ethnic Turks. In 2009, soft power hardened when then-foreign minister Ahmet Davutoglu intervened in a local political dispute, much to the Serbian government's anger. On buildings and walls just out-side the centre of the town 'INDEPENDENT SANDŽAK' is scrawled in graffiti; many of the residents resent Serbian rule and wish to revert to the city-state identity they held during the Ottoman era. Strangely, here, in the twenty-first century, the local desire for greater political indepen-dence is based in nostalgia for long-gone Ottoman-subject status.

In Novi Pazar, I conducted one of the most bizarre interviews of my life with Alija Šahović, the president of the Novi Pazar branch of the 'Friends of Sandžak'. I had first tried to track down the group's headquar-ters via Facebook – I sent a message in Turkish, and received a response in Turkish, inviting me to come and visit. Then, when I tried to ask about precise directions, I found myself inexplicably blocked.

I decided to go anyway, based on the map shown on the Facebook page, but could find no trace of the place in the sleepy river-side neigh-bourhood. As I stood rather helplessly outside a butcher's shop strung with calf carcasses, a 16-year-old boy wandered out. To my relief, he spoke excellent English thanks to a passion for American films and agreed to help me. 'I don't want a salary,' he said solemnly. 'But you must buy some beef sausage from my father's shop – no pork, we are Muslims here. My name is Elhan, by the way, pleasedtameetcha.'

After an hour of knocking on doors, a middle-aged bald man with a large beak of a nose poked his head out of the upper window of one house. 'What do you want?' he demanded, the tone of the Serbian words quite clear. This was Alija Šahović, and this was his house, aka the HQ of the Friends of Sandžak. He answered my Turkish greeting in kind, so I continued my pleasantries, only to be informed by Elhan that Šahović could not actually speak Turkish – the local version of Serbian had incor-porated a few Turkish words since Ottoman times, hence my confusion.

'We took Turkish words, like *merhaba*, and masturbated them into Serbian,' declared Elhan. I kept a straight face so that he would continue to translate for me, craning his head up at the upper window where Šahović's nose still poked out, warily.

'Alija apologises for blocking you on Facebook – he was worried you were a Gülenist,' Elhan told me. A Gülenist is a term for a follower of Fetullah Gülen, the cleric-enemy of the Turkish state. I had no idea why Šahović thought a Gülenist might be trying to infiltrate his group, but his attitude mirrored the paranoia of Turks in the aftermath of the attempted coup. Apparently, he had translated my message and sent a reply with the help of a Serbian friend based in Turkey, who, as an after-thought, advised him to block me. I think I was the first non-Serb to ever contact the group.

Assured that I had honest intentions, Šahović led us round to the back door through his garden. To my surprise, the terrace was strung with AKP bunting – Turkey's ruling political party – and large flags with President Erdoğan's face on them. We went into the house, where Šahović showed me further stashes of AKP bunting and stationery, Turkish Korans, and even AKP-branded versions of the decorative wands wielded at Turkish circumcision ceremonies – an extravaganza of nationalist merchandise packed into boxes in his basement because there was not enough space to display it all in his house.

Upstairs, my host insisted on fetching me tea prepared in the Turkish style, leading me into the kitchen to show me the samovar. 'Türk çay!' he said proudly, beaming as I accepted my tulip-shaped glass. In the sitting room, we sat on a leather sofa in front of a flat-screen television showing TRT, a Turkish state news channel – incomprehensible to Šahović, but he enjoyed having it playing constantly in the background, and occasionally being treated to the sight of Erdoğan's face.

I was overwhelmed by this Serbian man's passion for the modern reincarnation of the empire that had subjugated his ancestors. It was almost as though he was suffering from a historic case of Stockholm syndrome— a version of the 'Make America/Britain Great Again' nostalgia, but from the point of view of the colonised, rather than the coloniser. Why did he felt such an affinity for Turks?

'He thinks everyone should feel Turkish because the Ottomans made us, they gave us Islam,' Elhan translated. Apparently, Šahović considered himself, fundamentally, a Turk. Not so long ago, his family members grew up under Ottoman rule, speaking Turkish.

'Alija's mother's grandfather knew Turkish as well as Serbian,' said Elhan. 'And his wife's grandfather only knew Turkish. Here, until 1912, Turkish was the native language.'

Šahović was clearly regretful that he himself could speak only Serbian, which he insisted on calling 'Sanjakian'. Listening to him desperately try to convey his admiration for President Erdoğan, I was struck by how powerful Turkish influence had become in this region during the last fifteen years of Erdoğan's rule and in particular, how important the Islamic element of Šahović's self-invented identity is. Before Erdoğan's Justice and Development Party (AKP) took power in 2003, no Turkish government had been so explicitly religious – indeed, most were much more secular. Erdoğan has been the first Turkish leader to skilfully and unashamedly wield the Muslim card in pursuing a foreign policy which seeks to resuscitate an Ottoman sphere of influence. This has been the case not just in the Balkans but east of Turkey too. Palestine is an important case in point, where support for Erdoğan rocketed after he sent aid to Gaza in 2010, sparking a diplomatic rupture with Israel which still has not healed. On a recent trip to Palestine, I saw his face on posters in newsagents, and spoke to Palestinians who were delighted to hear of my Turkish heritage, gushing their support for a leader they expected me to venerate too, and explicitly citing his similarity to Ottoman sultans of old. The Muslim card is the common denominator between the Ottomans and the Turks – the denominator which Atatürk had temporarily erased when he created a secular Republic, and which Erdoğan effortlessly re-introduced shortly after he came to power, knowing it would have resonance far beyond Turkey's borders.

For Šahović, the Christian Serbs were oppressors, and the Turks were true and rightful overlords. 'Serbia is pushing out the Turkish influence,' he told me, seemingly oblivious to the last century of history. As I left, I asked him to pose for a photograph in front of the flags in his garden. He stood, proudly, making the Islamic Rabbi'ah sign adopted by Erdoğan when he addresses his rallies of the faithful – right hand held aloft, fingers spread, thumb tucked in. Here was my last image of what I am certain is the most historically confused 55-year-old fanboy I will ever encounter.

To get from Novi Pazar to Kosovo, you have to drive via Montenegro, because Serbia regards Kosovo not as an independent state but as Serbian territory occupied since the war of 1999, during which NATO forces intervened to stop the killing of the country's large ethnic Albanian contingent by Serb forces. The route is incredibly dramatic – up and down winding, heavily wooded mountain roads, via suspicious border post guards who demand unnecessary $15 'insurance' to let you pass. The Kosovan landscape is flat, a kind of war-ravaged basin encircled by hills. In the Ottoman town of Peja or Peć, near the Montenegran border, men sell flags depicting maps of Kosovo with wildly ambitious borders, encompassing Sandžak, Albania and even Corfu – a kind of fantasy Albanian mini-empire. In each sub-section of the Balkans, I was to find imagined borders and unique, self-declared identities such as this.

A few hours southeast of Peja is Prizren, a beautiful town dominated by a citadel and a lofty Orthodox church, since 1999 cordoned off and sporadically guarded by KFOR (NATO's Kosovo Force). Mosques and churches throughout Kosovo were targets during the war; the church in Prizren town was torched and a gloomy Serbian guard told me that the tiny Christian community was 'dead' – his church had become a lacklustre tourist attraction, not a functioning place of worship. Outside, a sign obscured by deep scratches proclaimed: 'This building site is protected by law. Any act of vandalism and looting will be considered a criminal offence of the utmost gravity.' In the town centre, KFOR soldiers patrolled, albeit in an aimless fashion, and from the Byzantine citadel above the town I watched Black Hawk helicopters circle – the stern eye of the West still obvious amid simmering tensions nearly twenty years after the conflict.

Unsurprisingly, Western powers are in no hurry to leave a strategic position so close to Russia, either militarily or otherwise, and court it accordingly. Despite being a war-ravaged disputed territory, Kosovo is a candidate member state of the EU and uses the Euro. I noticed that when I passed over the border my mobile phone, which did not work in Serbia, suddenly welcomed me to Slovenia – generous provider of mobile network coverage in Kosovo. American influence is strong too, as the primary force within KFOR. I tried (and failed) to get into an American army base outside Prishtina, the improbably named Camp Bondsteel, and chatted to the soldiers as I waited outside.

'The Kosovans seems to like you,' I said, remarking on the abundance of American flags flying from ordinary civilian homes.

'They'd better,' said a red-haired soldier with a Texan drawl. 'They wouldn't be here if it wasn't for us.'

Turkey is very much the new kid on the block in this scrum of imperial powers, but currently the most visible one. The seventeenth-century Sinan Pasha mosque 50 metres away from the vandalised church in Prizren has been restored to its former glory by TIKA money, according to a brass plaque bearing the Turkish flag and seal of the Turkish presidency; an Albanian-language newspaper claimed the renovations cost 1.2 million euros. Inside, as I gazed up at the calligraphy on the inside dome of the Sinan Pasha mosque, a young man came up to me, sensing I was not a local. He addressed me in English, but on an impulse, I answered in Turkish.

'You speak Turkish!' he exclaimed. 'Yes', I said. '... As do you?'

Ilaz, as he introduced himself, was visiting family in Kosovo, having settled in Switzerland, in common with many Kosovans who had fled there during the war. He explained that most people in Prizren had spoken Turkish since Ottoman times, having not been as effectively 'Serbified' as the inhabitants of Novi Pazar, including the unfortunate Alija Šahović. To me, someone used to standard mainland Turkish, the version that had persisted in Prizren sounded like a peculiar dialect. Later, I spoke to a newsagent who compared it to the Turkish spoken by people in the Black Sea – not a separate language as such, but with idiosyncratic pronunciations and grammar. He introduced proudly himself as Unal – 'a totally Turkish name'. He claimed that the 'modern' Turkish he and I were speaking was different to what he spoke at home with his family, and which I heard snippets of as he spoke to his daughter on the phone – 'it is an old Turkish, Ottoman.' This seemed to me a romantic view of what was essentially a dialect typical of the region – I could discern no archaic words, just an odd pronunciation, but what was interesting was that Unal *thought* he was speaking Ottoman. Remembering Šahović's adoration of Erdoğan, I asked him about his views on Turkish politics.

'We are just happy that Turkey is strong at the moment. No doubt if we lived in Turkey we would support some party or other. My relatives live in Izmir, they like the CHP [Turkey's main opposition party] – but as it is, we just like the fact that Turkey is strong. It's like supporting Turkey in a football game – you don't care which club the individual players are from. You just support Turkey.'

His analogy stayed with me – here was a more long-standing feeling of kinship than Šahović's frenzied worship of Erdoğan's brand, and I believe the key to this was language: Turkish had been spoken here in Kosovo since time immemorial, so a feeling of affinity with Turkey was not linked solely to religion or politics (although, admittedly, Turkey's perceived ascendance under Erdoğan's rule made it more attractive, like a star striker enhancing a national team). Kosovo is, ironically, less politicised than Serbia, in the sense that it is more or less homogenously Muslim, as opposed to a Christian state with a fiercely independent and resentful Muslim demographic in the south. In Serbia, Turkey can exploit ethno-religious tensions and promote Turko-Islamic identity in people like Alija Šahović; in Kosovo, a sense of Ottoman heritage is well-established, without the zeal of a recent awakening.

A few kilometres outside Prizren is the most Turkish enclave of Kosovo: Mamusha (originally 'Mahmut Pasha'), the only ethnic Turk-majority town in Kosovo. A gate at the entrance of the town welcomes you in Turkish: 'Hoşgeldiniz', with the Albanian and English signs underneath, almost as afterthoughts. Its streets are lined with car part replacement stores, garages and kebab houses full of mechanics eating lunch. Unlike in Prizren, I heard no Albanian at all. I also saw no women—a young man I met in the park told me they come out at weddings and *bayrams* (festivals). A wedding party passed by as I walked down the main street an hour later, cars trailing white and red streamers, horns honking incessantly and women waving shyly from inside the cars.

In Mamusha the Erdoğan brand is big, as in southern Serbia, due largely to ties created with Turkey by the Mayor, Arif Butuç, who welcomed Erdoğan in 2010 to open the 'Anatolia' primary school, and who supported him through the anti-government Gezi Park protests in 2013. The local park is full of benches with 'Keçiören' painted onto the wood – obviously donated by Keçiören Municipality in Ankara. It is as if the town itself has been branded, and the locals are more than happy with that. 'We are Turks, from long ago,' a waiter in the Genç Osman ('Young Ottoman') restaurant told me. I asked him if he felt Kosovan. 'My heart is Turkish.'

On 23 July, shortly after my visit, the Ottoman Tomato Festival would be celebrated with much pomp and ceremony – 'flags and drums, there is a big procession,' the young man in the park told me. 'Turkish vegetable suppliers come and try the tomatoes, then they pick the best ones and order imports. We produce many tonnes of tomatoes.' An extensive internet search revealed no such Ottoman tomato tradition, which meant that a local trade festival had been retrospectively 'Ottomanised' and jazzed up from maximum nationalistic impact – no surprises there.

From Kosovo, I headed south to the Republic of Macedonia, home of Alexander the Great and historically troublesome neighbour to both Serbia and Bulgaria. Unlike much of the Balkans, where the countryside is dominated either by Muslim or Christian villages, Macedonia is dotted with churches and mosques in quick succession. The country felt surprisingly Soviet, its street signs in Cyrillic, and socialist housing blocks even in the villages. On the banks of Lake Ohrid, hotels built in the 1960s reminded me of abandoned Soviet holiday homes on the banks of Lake Sari-Chelek in Kyrgyzstan – one of the other limited holiday destinations for Russians during the Cold War. The Ottoman past life of Ohrid itself, traditionally known as the 'Jerusalem of the Balkans', is obvious in its distinctive white houses with black-edged windows next to the remaining Byzantine churches. The overwhelming air is of a once-magical town gone to seedy tourism.

Macedonia's capital, Skopje, was conquered by the Ottomans in 1392 and remained under its control until 1912, when Macedonia joined the Balkan League in fighting for independence from the Empire. After a massive municipal splurge in 2013, the visible narrative of the city is strikingly anti-Ottoman; gargantuan bronze statues of Balkan nationalist heroes like Gotse Delchev, Pavel Satev, Hristo Tatarchev, Vasil Cakalarov and Boris Sarafov, who led rebellions against the Ottomans at the turn of the twentieth century, dominate the centre, alongside similarly enormous statues of Alexander the Great and some inexplicable bronze horses bursting upwards out of a monstrous fountain. But, like Prizren, Skopje's social Ottoman legacy is still strong – around 10 per cent of the community are ethnic Turks, concentrated on the eastern bank of the River Vardar, and even non-Turks speak the language brokenly. The signs on mosques are in Turkish, as is random graffiti – 'Özlem [a girl's name] – I'm so sorry,' declared one anguished, love-struck message on a garage door. In the old Ottoman bazaar, now given up almost entirely to tourists, I passed one baklava shop with an enormous, faded poster of Erdoğan's relatively youthful face, called 'Turkish Angela Merkel Baklava' – presumably established in the height of the political romance between the two leaders circa 2011 (and sadly lapsed since then). A short away from the bazaar, I found peaceful little tea gardens such as one finds across Turkey, with old men sitting and chatting in Turkish over endless glasses of tea. Like Sarajevo, Turkish tourists throng the streets, and the Turkish lira-Macedonian denar exchange rate is displayed prominently at the top of the bureau de change.

By this point in my travels, I had made a realisation: nouveau-Ottomanism is not purely a construct of Erdoğan's, or the AKP's. Muslims in the Balkans are aware of their Ottoman heritage and already identify with Turkey – there is a ghost empire here ripe for the taking and it just needed to be brought to life.

Erdoğan knew this when he entered power in 2002. He was aware of the realpolitik advantages of resurrecting influence in the region, especially for trade, but there has always been a more emotional impetus behind this: Erdoğan identifies as an Ottoman leader in troubled modern times, leading the faithful. Sometimes he signals this with heavy-handed symbolism, sitting in his newly-built, 1,000-room White Palace in Ankara with all the trappings of a modern sultan, and other times vocally, such as when he lamented the precise loss of Ottoman territories at the fall of the Empire in 1923.

'In 1914, our land covered 2.5 million square kilometres. Nine years later it fell to 780,000 square kilometres.'

'Our land' is the key: Erdoğan and the fellow founders of the AKP both assume and actively promote a political continuum between the Ottoman Empire and modern Turkey. During the liberation of Mosul in 2016, Turkish state TV channels broadcast maps of a new, enlarged Turkey encompassing northern Iraq, an old Ottoman territory. If the Balkans were as militarily vulnerable, perhaps the map would include those territories too. As it is, the Turks are playing it softly in the west.

MERYL PUGH

THE TALK

gridlock all afternoon   some parts of Luton
just aren't passable   not since the fens went under
and what with pirates and illegal downloads
nothing's stopping at Epping   who would any more?
boar literally   everywhere on the island

and all the mosquitos   they're picking coal off the beach
at Morecambe   there was a minke whale but it died
and when I got there   it was nothing but plastic
I had to wear carrier bags on my feet
all the furniture's gone off to the dump

the party had a crasher   did I mention the shoes?
I like a cappuccino at eleven
then I might hit the shops   you have to fight
your way through the crowds but it's worth it
wait is this the house? this isn't the house

you'd better hope no one was in at the time
don't go to hospital, no one's there   but the woman
down Hartley Road knows where to get some   I fixed
the kettle because I'm like I'M HAVING A COFFEE
and all this pale muck came out   we want all students

to feel safe   number twenty-six
got carted off last night   she never hurt no one
but that's what I'm saying   are you being torn apart?
is someone you know at risk?   our lollipop lady's
a PhD, aren't we all?   do you believe

in God or do you believe in shopping?   of course
when you reach that level you just don't do you?
take the next right   turn right   crossroads ahead
concealed exit   what's on the other side?
many gifts for the children we'll find out soon

CICADA

After the engines: the echo-less quiet of Arrivals.

Flat green, grey roads, an avenue of trees.

No shadows – no, everything a shadow.

What a conundrum, this new, sharper atmosphere.
        It will not admit the creek, fast water over a shallow bed.
        It will not admit the pavement, steaming after rain.
        It rips away the shadow, moving over the cloud
                under continuous blue.

A blank space, a question mark, split
        carapace, wobbling form.

5 POSTCARDS

The Avenue: a double row of shrubs.
Two goshawks tumble round each other, crows
keep company with gulls around the goalposts.
Real horses pass, a vixen pelts away.

*

I thought it was a sack and brown bees hovering
but they were flies, the cat was dead, his hind legs
folded under neatly: a winter coat.
That helicopter's low, can't see it either.

*

A pit bull barrels down the bridleway
to rootle out a mangled tennis ball,
a couple of cans, an apple core, a bag
of chicken bones and nappies from the bin.

*

'Dear Bess, Just a card to tell you
Mrs C wants me to stay until Friday
so will make it about the same time Friday
evening instead of Wednesday. Much love, Lily.'

*

Against the Quakers' wall (spraypainted brick)
she looks away, his face is in her hair.
Inside the wood: a clearing, a marshy pond,
the mallard pair tucked between the rushes.

CHRIS SUCCO

PLATES

ART

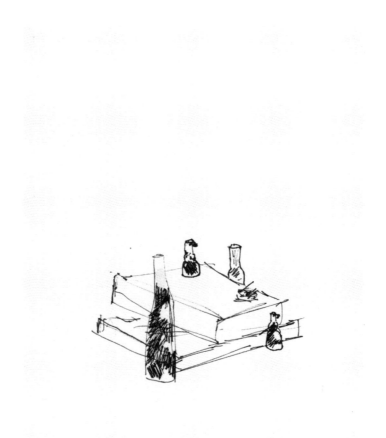

XXIII

THE HORROR
SASCHA MACHT
tr. AMANDA DEMARCO

'A man from Skagafjörðr dreamed he came into a great house where two women were rocking. They were covered with blood, and blood rained on the windows.'   Eliot Weinberger, *An Archeology of Dreams*

The island where I was born rose from the cold, sombre depths of the ocean in the 1940s. Volcanic activity and tectonic tremors brought about by US nuclear arms testing suddenly brought forth a new nation in a forgotten corner of the globe: blazing peaks, barren steppes, whispering bluffs, and colourful swamps. Grasses thrived, little trees twisted skyward, shrubbery spread. The island was already inhabited by white bees, carnivorous flightless birds, and natatory mammals when the first human set foot on it, perhaps a modern pirate, an ornithologist come unhinged, an awol soldier, or a scion of the European oligarchy wandering the seas in his yacht. An ancient and peculiar fragment of earth had emerged from the waters which had swallowed it millions of years earlier, a threadbare republic was born and then annihilated, the wind swept over the beach, a fruit bat shrieked, someone reached for someone else's hand.

In the days when my island once again faced perdition, I had just turned 17 and had decided to dedicate my little scrap of future solely and completely to those horror films that took my breath away and inexorably robbed me of my sleep as well as my reason. I was a great admirer of Marcel Kürten's slender body of works, a terrifying sequence of films in which animals, plants, and objects take on human form under the influence of cosmic forces and wreak havoc on their surroundings. I was also mad about the works of Israeli director Jael Guldenburg, which all took place in forbidding locations: on the floor of the Dead Sea, on a distant, darksome planet made of smoothly polished metal, in the labyrinthine cellar system of a skyscraper in the middle of the desert, on a cruise ship adrift forever in the endlessness of the Pacific Ocean, on the fringe of an icy terrain inhabited by fur-covered giants with red eyes, or in the inflamed abdominal cavity of a dying man. Roberto Madrigal's short flicks made me downright dizzy, reinterpretations of Japanese ghost stories in which groups of simple people converged by chance and had to ward off uncanny figures that had moulted from the husk of an age-old nature, emerging from singing streams, dense underbrush, the hollow interior of a green hill, or a dank trench in the earth.

I owned all of these films and many more. I'd arranged the VHS tapes on a shelf and I looked at them again and again, after getting up in the morning, at lunch, on hot afternoons, and in the deep of the night when I couldn't sleep. Now and again, I paid a visit to Handsome Hans, proprietor of a tiny shop operated under the Beauty & Hope franchise. Along with personal hygiene products from Soviet reserves, trench coats, Bulgarian cigarettes, cans of tinned food, old TV guides, and hairpieces, he also sold video cassettes: Hollywood classics, pornos, Latin American TV series, anime and horror films. Trucks from western relief agencies drove the goods across the island, armed bandits from the surrounding hills and forests ambushed the convoys and hawked the goods to people like Handsome Hans, who stocked his shop with them. Mostly he just gave me the films I wanted for free. I was the only one interested in them anyway.

Bruno, he would say, take that crap and go, I don't want it on my shelves any more.

The village where I grew up was called Kajagoogoo. It was founded in 1989, as the sallow candlelight of communism began to wane in the rest of the world, by my parents and a handful of their friends as a sort of New Age refuge at the end of history. Those were the days when the governments on my island lasted half a year, the nationalists ousted by the socialists, the socialists by the liberals, the liberals by the last communists, and the last communists by the nationalists once again. No one in the nearby provincial capital of Savannah or the more distant national capital cared one whit that somewhere in the wilderness, a village had been founded, which is how my parents managed to go on largely unchecked at the edge of the Great Savannah, the dead eye of a hurricane that the politicians of our island whipped into a frenzy in the years that followed.

When I was 14, my father gave me a camcorder that he'd stolen from a Norwegian backpacker who'd passed through our village. It was a simple thing with a flat, hinged screen and mini-cassettes that I could only play back on our television after a special video recorder appeared in Hans's shop, which he gave to me after I'd done drudge work there for a year. I could edit the films after another tourist, a Spaniard, Chilean or Argentine (no one really knew) spent a lonely night in our village and was forced to continue on without his laptop. From then on nothing could hold me back: I filmed the landscape around the village, the sunrises and sunsets, the wind that shook the brush, the cattle in the pastures, the rabbits and deer in the forests, the fish in the river, and the swallows in the sky. I recorded the inhabitants of the village at their work, the cars that drove along the federal road in the distance, the heaps of trash piled up everywhere, and the rats that rummaged in them. At night, I superimposed my voice on the images using the laptop, recounting whatever had happened to me lately, without it having anything to do with what I'd filmed. Later I left the sound out entirely, because the images seemed increasingly foreign and inscrutable, and I was uncertain if they really depicted what I'd seen, although it did seem to be daily life in our village that they showed. So really, I was keeping a film diary more than I was practising filmmaking. I didn't develop my fascination with horror until after my parents had disappeared.

The night my parents didn't return to Kajagoogoo was the night before my sixteenth birthday. Now and then the two of them took the bus to the provincial capital in the morning to take care of something or other, clear their heads, or spend time together, but they always came back early in the evening with a little gift for me. That day, nothing indicated that they wouldn't return: my mother prepared the provisions for the journey while my father told me I should round up the chickens when it got dark, but they would probably be back long before that. I filmed them as they left our house and set out down the road to the bus stop, my mother in her long grey dress, my father with a straw hat on his head and a shopping bag in his hand as they walked down the dusty, sunlit street past the fountain, Handsome Hans's shop and the caravan park. When I couldn't see them any more, I went back into the house, lay down in my bed, and for the first time recorded myself while masturbating, a strange, nervous feeling, composed of curiosity, braggadocio, and shame. I spent the rest of the day filming in the house, and in the evening I sat in front of the laptop and didn't recognise any of the images flickering on the display. I went to bed around 2, excited about my birthday and surprised that my parents weren't back yet. That morning I didn't find any trace of them in the house. The chickens weren't there either, because I'd forgotten to lock them behind their gate. I ate a banana for breakfast, drank coffee, and stared out of the window. A few villagers were out and about, clearing away clutter, sweeping their doorsteps, or standing stiffly at the edge of the street looking at the ground. I filmed them through the dirty windowpane, then went down into the village to ask about the whereabouts of the last bus.

It drove on yesterday, said Handsome Hans, even on time for a change.

I explained that my parents hadn't come home.

Handsome Hans shrugged his shoulders and said I should relax, my parents were dauntless hippies in the depths of their very souls, and surely they were lying somewhere arm-in-arm with a couple of other naked people in a big bed, sleeping off their high.

I asked Hans if he could repeat that, and if I could film him doing it, but he chased me off.

The months that followed passed in a flash: people left the village to seek their fortunes elsewhere, a few old people died, a few children were born, sometimes the weather was bad, but often the sun simply shone and nothing happened. Just after my parents' disappearance, I occupied myself with news from other parts of the island, listened to the radio, or read the daily anarchist newspaper, *Chinese Lantern*. That's how I learned of the overthrow of the 12-year-old chief of state Immanuel Sullus by his Vice-President Emmy Jaeger, who had managed to draw the military to her side; of the surprising declaration of independence on the part of the northwestern mountain province, which wasn't recognised by the central government; and of the crumbling of our Republican society, which really wasn't a crumbling any more, but rather a full-blown collapse, as some commentators were convinced. Not only did the Republic seem to be home to rich people, of whom there were never many, there were also very many poor people whose numbers were skyrocketing; and along with these poor and rich people, there were a few renegade governors who were in league with criminal syndicates in the countryside and had seized command of small parts of the various provinces like crazed warlords. When I heard one day that Ex-President Sullus had also disappeared without a trace, I gave up on following the malevolent politics of my island because I had come to understand that my parents' disappearance and Ex-President Sullus's disappearance were akin to a black lagoon whose bottom can't be seen for the sole reason that the revolutionaries from the mountains, the Republican politicians, the gangster bosses in the blighted villages, or whoever, had dumped thousands upon thousands of tons of shit into its water. In addition, I stopped filming my surroundings and ornamenting them with my silence because I no longer had any desire to depict reality without comment – it was far too vain and opaque for that. If I wanted to continue filming, and I did, more than anything else, then I had to find a way to come to grips with this reality, to put it in its place, to hurl all of the hatred and rage of my youthful existence at it in the hope that it would shatter and something would emerge from behind it. I was miserable as a dog, couldn't sleep, sobbed and shrieked alone in the house, and smashed the furniture. If I hadn't stumbled upon the horror films of Marcel Kürten, Jael Guldenburg, Roberto Madrigal, Natalia van Vijfeijken, Jim Wu, Alejandro Filippo Zeissiger, Ferenc Lima and Terrence Nadongo in Hans's shop, then who knows, sooner or later maybe I would have taken the final freight elevator to the stars, as my mother would have put it.

Handsome Hans kept the video cassettes in a box toward the back of his store. They'd come in a goods donation from Europe, a shipping container full of all sorts of stuff. The bandits that he bought the donation from insisted that he take everything, not just the things he was sure to be able to sell in the village. During one of my forays in search of clothing and edible items, he called me over from afar, led me into the storeroom, and showed me the box.

Take a look, maybe there's something for you in there? he asked.

We kneeled and rummaged through the box.

What's that? I asked and looked at Hans with my reddened eyes.

Just movies, weird stuff. *The Dead University. The Cockroaches of Phrygia. The Rats of Dalmatia. 3 Short Films: Contrabasists - Leather Men - Hewers of Flesh. Bulbin the Demolisher. SS Standarte Zombie II.* And so on. Heard of any of it?

No.

Me neither. Looks pretty bottom-of-the-barrel. You can have it, if you want. I'll be getting more in soon, I'm afraid.

I nodded, picked up the box, and carried it outside.

Listen, Bruno, said Hans.

Mhm?

Nothing. Don't worry about it.

I spent the next day screening the material. All of it was appallingly bad, the sound incomprehensible, the images shaky, the effects cheap, and the actors beastly. Quite a few of them seemed to be acute alcoholics, or to be acting under the influence of hard drugs. Mostly the films were black-and-white. Some simply stopped in the middle of a sentence without any narrative justification, though I suspected that the directors had simply run out of money. And yet they made a deep impression on me, a sort of perspective into an alien and threatening world, independent of but not infinitely far from my daily reality of looking for food, brooding for hours, needing to sleep, and dreaming brief, gruesome dreams; a black, shattered mirror that showed everything that wasn't, everything that had been long, long ago, or would only be in the future. I was particularly taken with *Leather Men* by Marcel Kürten, I must have watched it thirty times: a solar flare caused all leather items on earth to take on human proportions, becoming beings with creased, quadratic heads, zippered mouths, and long arms that ended in sharp hooks; suddenly they're everywhere, hiding in dark corners, standing motionless in the street, or creeping through the forest, but no one can talk to them or understand what they have to say. They're not dangerous, nearly pitiable in their thick-wittedness, but the people still decide to revert the beings to their original forms in huge factories, to make them into handbags, wallets, shoes, saddles, jackets, gloves, and soccer balls again. An enormous slaughter begins, at the end of which the leather men gain the upper hand and, in turn, they transform the bodies of the human population into everyday items: chairs, tables, cupboards, houses, and decorative elements.

In the time that followed, I thought about many important things: What would my future be like? Would I stay in Kajagoogoo forever? What had happened to Marcel Kürten, Alejandro Filippo Zeissiger, Roberto Madrigal, and all the others? Besides me, was there anyone else in the world who watched their films? What effects would the ongoing consumption of this dreadful, overwhelmingly nauseating, cynical, fascistic drivel wreak on my young soul? At that moment, I couldn't answer a single one of my questions, and so I procured four new chickens from old Madame Ilyuschina's barnyard, in order to have fresh eggs each morning.

Soon Handsome Hans gave me another box of films from a ship's cargo that had been transported hundreds of kilometres inland only to fall into the hands of bandits just before reaching its destination. It included a few sequels, Zeissinger's *Return to the Dead University*, Nadongo's *Bulbin Mows Them All Down!*, and Lima's *SS Standarte Zombie, Parts III - VII*, but also films by a few directors still unfamiliar to me: Junior Galante, Donata Michalczuk, Sabine Oslov, Eddie from Outer Space, Buster Lee, the Bulli siblings, and X Wohlff. It was hard for me to tell when the films had been made; often they were so simple and dilettantish that they could well have had seventy or eighty years under their belts, or been quickly filmed yesterday. It also occurred to me to watch something different for a change, maybe something like *When Harry Met Sally...*, *Gladiator*, *Star Trek V: The Final Frontier*, *The Bodyguard*, or *Rain Man*, all of which stood at the very front of Hans's video stand in their original packaging. I watched them all, but soon I returned to my agonising drivel, which seemed to be able to provide me with something that none of the big productions could: that sense of speechless wonder that is sometimes borne of financial as well as intellectual limitation.

Incidentally, for the first time in my life, I began to take conscious note of the people around me: sometimes I had long conversations with Handsome Hans, whom I'd known for as long as I could remember but had never taken an interest in. I learned that he'd lived for a few years in the capital of the Republic and had moved to the countryside to be safe after he was forced to learn the hard way about the secret service's intrigues.

I've caused a lot of people a lot of pain, and a lot of people have caused me a lot of pain, he said and stared for a long time at a point in the distance. After that, he didn't want to talk about it anymore.

Madame Ilyuschina taught me to care for animals. Although I still only had my four chickens, she explained to me how to help a cow birth its calf, how to teach an ape to steal, how to train a falcon to dive at other people on command, how to correctly kill a goat in such a way as to spill the least blood possible, what pigs eat (not everything, but a little of everything), the conditions that promote the well-being of armadillos, and how to make swans do what you require of them. Her granddaughter Lissa was my age, and we slept together twice, once on the floor of my room and the other time in a dry creek bed outside of Kajagoogoo, but I quickly lost interest in her and she in me.

There was another boy in the village, Perry Hartwig, who I spent my free time with, and I had plenty of it. I mostly watched him fire his air pistol, or listened to his jokes, which he invented himself: short, boring stories or just punchlines. Perry tore off screaming after we'd watched the first fifteen minutes of Ferenc Lima's *Sweet Slaughterhouse, Mon Amour*. Later he apologised to me, he had a weak stomach but as a matter of principle he was open to all forms of art. After that, I showed him Donata Michalczuk's *Lovely Bodies, Red Nights, Blind Worms* and had to call his parents over to push Perry's unconscious body home in a wheelbarrow.

I began to carry out renovations on the house. I replaced the gutters, oiled the hinges on the front door, sanded the boards of the veranda smooth, patched the decrepit water heater with burnt rice porridge, and got the garden ship-shape again. In the forest, I found a few pieces of furniture in good condition: two chairs, a guest bed, a dresser, and a kitchen table, and I distributed them through the rooms of my house. What's more, at the edge of the savanna, I found a small green car that I broke into and hot wired. At first I wanted to drive it into the ground, but instead I parked it in the driveway so that maybe someday I could finally get out of here.

I began to film again tentatively. I concentrated on details, recorded my breakfast eggs bursting in boiling water, a chicken shitting, the skin under my chin where stubble was beginning to sprout, filth that accumulated in the corners of rooms, the faucet dripping in the kitchen, a mosquito entangled in a spiderweb. The certainty that I would someday have to make my own horror film to keep from going crazy hung at the back of my mind like a leery, black gossamer cocoon.

One night I sat around for a long time in the living room, and since I couldn't sleep, I turned on the national television station. The news at 2.30 in the morning consisted of a montage of former grade school teacher and current President Emmy Jaeger's vacation memories, how she went for walks on the beach with her family, how she smiled tiredly as she shoved a gourd into the mouth of an aged elephant, how she rambled like a masked phantom through the ruins of a multi-family residence destroyed in a terror attack, how she silently and severely pointed at the grey sea with an outstretched arm, toward the sunset, as if something were hidden out there that must be found, a ship lost in a storm, a mythical monstrosity capable of swallowing all of the enemies of the Republic together, or a small island inhabited only by a herd of silent apes who sat, day in, day out, in the shadow of a sandalwood tree observing the motion of the waves.

I received the third box just before Christmas, a quarter of a year after my parents' disappearance. At first Handsome Hans refused to give it to me. He'd become concerned that the films were drawing me inexorably downward into a whirlpool of insanity, and he didn't want to hand them over anymore. I explained to him in a serious tone that I had long been swimming for my life at the edge of that whirlpool, and that these films were the only thing that kept me from giving up. Hans replied that one shouldn't confuse the whirlpool of insanity with the whirlpool of false hope, though both led inevitably to the floor of the very same hushed, empty ocean, from which there was no escape. But then we both were forced to admit that we had wandered carelessly into a thicket of sanctimonious metaphors, and Hans handed me the box shaking his head. This time there were many films I already knew and possessed in my collection, along with a few sequels and three cassettes whose ribbons I thought were damaged, as they only showed a black expanse with points of lights in it, streaked with perfectly straight white lines that sometimes drifted across the screen from bottom to top, sometimes from top to bottom. Only the film *Sun Hours* by Adelaide Turner left me paralysed before the television for days, a five-hour-long ordeal that took place in near total darkness, in which hundreds of figures, unrecognisable either as people or as something else, searched for a mysterious object, which in their shrill conversations, they sometimes designated as Escape Stone, sometimes as Sour Nectar of Hermeneutics, sometimes as Unfamiliar Gender. After I had watched the film for the fourth time, I jumped around in the house, laughed, screamed, and drummed around on the furniture, because I was struck by the sudden, forceful realisation that I had fallen in love for the first time. It didn't matter to me, though, that I didn't know if I had fallen in love with the director Adelaide Turner, with her film, with the clumsy, babbling, helpless but nonetheless murderous creatures that appeared in it, or with the eternal darkness that surrounded them. Probably all of it together. I imagined that Marcel Kürten and Adelaide Turner got married and came to visit me in Kajagoogoo in order to adopt me, go for walks with me on the endless savanna, and sing me to sleep at night with their ice-cold voices.

I spent the first hours of the Christmas holiday alone, then went to Madame Ilyuschina's barnyard later. The people on my island had very particular ideas about Christmas Eve, which consisted in spending two whole days three sheets to the wind, shooting fireworks into the sky, and setting the trash heaps on fire, which is why in Kajagoogoo it was generally referred to as Night of the Burning Rats. In spring I discovered the joys and marvels of the internet when Handsome Hans showed me his new computer one day, the only one in the whole village with internet access. He wanted to establish a second source of income by converting half of his shop into an internet café, the future belonged to the new technology after all, every bonehead knew that. Several times per week I now hung around at Hans's, looking at horror film sites, rifling through horror film forums, and reading horror film reviews, and after a while I became rather well-informed about the biographies of my directors as well as their oeuvres, and I felt confirmed in the belief that I was really the only one who could actually enjoy these works. I also began preparations for my first feature film, *The Apprehension*, whose screenplay I had written over the winter, just five loose sheets, though I believed that they contained everything that was near to my heart at that time. I wanted to shoot the entire film on the savanna, just the sky and a narrow horizon of grass in the distance as a background. The constant murmuring of water would be audible throughout the entire length of the film, because the protagonists, a cannibal child, a cannibal teenager, a middle-aged cannibal, and a very, very old cannibal, would be completely convinced that they lived in a world that consisted only of miles-high waterfalls, rushing cascades, and boundless rapids on whose narrow rock ledges and under constant threat of obliteration, tiny pockets of infinitesimally few people had established their dwellings. I told Perry about my plans, but he couldn't understand why I was determined to shoot the film on the savanna and not by a river or lake or, for all he cared, at the edge of a big puddle.

Because it's a film about delusions, I explained. The cannibals believe that they're living in a world that doesn't really exist; they also believe that they are individual people of various ages and various mindsets, although all four of them are merely the likeness of a single person, and that person is me, Bruno Hidalgo.

Perry thought I was crazy, but promised to help me with the filming, though he himself had no desire to be in front of the camera.

And so I found myself confronted with the great problem of finding actors for my project, not suitable actors, but anyone, really, who would be prepared to perform. I would be able to talk Handsome Hans into it, of that I had no doubt. Perry persisted in his dogged refusal. I could cast Madame Ilyuschina as the old cannibal, if I could convince her to conceal her long straw-coloured hair under an enormous hat. I myself didn't want to perform, in the final sequence at most, when the tired eyes of the four cannibals become my own eyes, in which the savanna's blood red sea of grass is mirrored. Lissa would have been good as the teenaged cannibal, but I didn't know how she felt about me at that point; I had long believed that she fervently hated my obsessive passion, and since I hadn't stopped watching films, she had come to hate me too. In one of the caravans there lived a gaunt, bald-headed man by the name of E. T. the Extraterrestrial who could have played one of the older cannibals, but word in the village was that he was unpredictable and could be overcome at any second by bloodlust, which no one could quell. Perry's father Ignacio was the only other person who came to mind, but he was in a wheelchair because he had lost both legs during a brief stay at the detention centre in the provincial capital. I didn't know any of the other residents of Kajagoogoo well enough, or I considered them to be yellow-bellied rednecks who would rather die than act in a poetic cannibal film.

Soon summer hoisted its flag, and my project gradually went into the weeds. On top of that, my parents' savings, which I'd hidden in a shoebox in the bedroom, were slowly dwindling. I asked Handsome Hans if I could help him out for a while, but he said that business had been so bad lately that he was seriously considering burning his shop down to at least cash in on the small insurance payment from the Republican Cooperative. Since I couldn't think of any other way to support myself, I set up camp at the fountain, where I put my own furniture up for sale. Once I nearly managed to complete a transaction with E. T. the Extraterrestrial, but after he turned a vase wrathfully in his hands for a minute, staring and snorting into its dark mouth, I gave him the vessel for free and thanked him for his patronage. Three days later I brought everything back home because in the village no one gave a damn about me and the things that my parents had used before their disappearance. At night I sat at the kitchen table and wracked my little brain about how I could come into a large sum of money as quickly as possible without ruining the rest of my life. But it was no use: like so many other young people, I would have to drive my car to the provincial capital, Savannah, to try my luck.

OUT OF MY HANDS
MEGAN HUNTER

ESSAY

This baby is upside down. Today, they called her a *stargazer breech*, her head tipped up to a sky she has never seen, its curves nudging me through the skin of my stomach. On other days she is a stuck puppy, snagged in a tail-chase, lying horizontally across my body in a way they gently call *transverse*. They say this instead of noting the reality: that my stomach is an oblong, at these moments. That it has been stretched beyond all recognition.

*

Some women report that their brains open up like flowers when they are pregnant, dilating as their vaginas will, becoming large clear eyes to the world. Masterpieces have been written in pregnancy, I am sure of it.

But there is another group, perhaps the ones who never liked PE, who preferred to linger and gossip at the back. For us, pregnancy rolls over like a sea mist, obscuring everything. Even the outlines of our hands are indistinct. Every day, instead of wandering to the page, my mind seeks out the blanking, sweet relief of pregnancy porn. Name sites, and nutrition pages, shops where I buy sheets and bottles and tiny, tiny socks.

*

Some people believe that ideas are like ghosts or fairies, flitting around the world until they find the right mind. It happened to me before. Nothing, and then something. Creation *ex nihilo*: how God made the world, maybe.

Meanwhile, people keep asking me how I did it. *How was your book written*, they ask. *Why is it like that?*

*

I read about classic pregnancies. Adam, pregnant with Eve in his ribs. Mary, filled with Jesus, pregnant with joy. We wait for Him in Advent, the God books say, but that doesn't mean we do nothing. It is called *active waiting*.

When Sylvia Plath was pregnant, she compared herself to a house, a melon, a purse. The baby, when it came, was a fish, a slate, a bean. It was never a book.

*

Recently I have been travelling a lot, speaking about my work in rooms with bright lights, an amiable interrogation. Afterwards, I lumber my bulk into taxis, accepting the help of younger men who shut doors carefully behind me.

At some point, soft cheeks became vulnerable instead of attractive, baby-nice instead of sexy. These people are my children, I think. I am mother to the whole world. Delusion feels easier these days, almost cosy.

On stage, I always end up speaking about my first child while the second squirms. Sometimes, she kicks my book off my stomach where I have rested it, a convenient ledge.

Meanwhile, the firstborn rages. He doesn't want to go to nursery. He doesn't want to put on his shoes or listen to stories, those great advances of humankind. He has discovered death, and he is angry about it.

*

After bedtime, I spend many hours exchanging words with women who may be thousands of miles away, or not women at all. On these forums, we are bodies only, lines of blue, links of darker blue: aching backs, fatigue, babies whose limbs keep us up all night. Many of us have done it before, but this seems to make no difference: it is new every time.

Is this normal? we write over and over, teenagers again, bewildered by transformation.

*

In the mornings, the toddler looms his face over mine. When will you die? he asks me. When will I?

Is this normal?

*

My body begins to break open. Relaxin floods the blood, which pushes the pelvis apart. Making room, a geological process, forcing the cliffs to let the sea rush out.

My body makes more than the usual amount of relaxin. Or my bones can't cope with the usual amount. They don't know which. Instead of explanations, they offer hydrotherapy, which turns out to be a massive warm bath in the middle of the hospital. In the water I am joined by two women in their nineties who smile at my stomach beatifically, as though they can see the second coming.

From the poolside, a woman with a soft voice gives us the simplest of instructions: lift your leg. Bend your knee. Raise your arm five inches above your head and drop your wrist, like a ballerina. The elderly women do so, gracefully. I do so, shakily. I seem to have reached the place I wanted to go.

*

My best friend is having her third boy any day now. We want to look out of the window and see him gliding towards us on the east wind, like a balloon. We are watching for him.

One thing I can tell you, she says, and I turn towards her, listening, my face wide open to it, to anything. *One thing I can tell you: your first child will seem enormous.*

My first child's head, she explains, will swell and float above my hospital bed like a new kind of human. It will be a buoyant head, clear and mysteriously holding its own weight. I will, in just a few hours, have become used to the dense second head that lolls in my elbow like a compacted bowling ball. I will have become used to this.

My first child's head will seem enormous not only compared to my second child's head, she seems to be saying, but compared to heads in general, to any head you have ever seen. I will wonder that the human head can be so large, and floating, and still have such luminous skin.

*

This baby may not be born the normal way, the way that women have been doing it for all time, the way I did it with my first.

But I have been reading that normality is questionable, in light of our spindly, inadequate pelvises, in light of the great swelling of the human mind. The human mind has grown too big to fit through the human pelvis, which has not swelled enough in response.

And I did not get down in a cave and sweat and push my first out, glistening. I was hooked to a thousand machines. A man I was sure I knew from somewhere (the gym? the postman?) came in and inserted a needle into my back. I took his hands and gazed at him with a special kind of love, the kind you might reserve for a celebrity. *Thank you*, I said.

Is that not magic, to be able to turn agony off with a switch? Our swollen brains have surely accomplished something wonderful.

*

The new book begins and begins and begins and never ends. It is multiple universe theory, a world without edges.

It is the time that I was driven to the hospital at 3 or 4 in morning, dripping blood.

You are so melodramatic, my friends say. *You were not dripping blood.*

I was not dripping blood; I took care of myself. I was shown to various people who didn't know what to do with the sight of me. A tired young woman who pushed her gloved fingers inside and poked, as though trying to finish the job.

But in the blazing morning a large, scented woman placed a plastic disc on my stomach, and we heard an oncoming train, thunder, a galloping tsunami. A beat of life that filled the whole ward.

But that was the first child. He was tough.

*

All kinds of invisible things have been seen in our bodies: madness, love, imagination. I think if they scanned my brain they might see my future books in there, neural maps, the oldest words on Earth.

*

This time, in the dark, holy room, we found out about *she, her, a girl*. Three lines for female, they said, and I thought that seemed serpentine in nature, a sharp trinity.

*

The midwives and doctors have often not been able to tell the difference between a head and an arse. *It is surprising*, I say to my husband, *to learn that the two are so similar*. Even the experts have trouble telling them apart, running their fingers across the cleft over and over, frowning.

But today it is clear: her bottom is by my bottom, her top close to my top. There should not be this compatibility: they should be opposites. And so, the doctor informs me, they will have to try and turn the baby with their bare hands. They will hold me down to a table, he says, and they will twist so hard their faces will turn red.

Baby likes to have her head close to your heart, the midwife says nicely when it all fails. The doctor has pushed himself into a corner; he is breathless, his forehead reflective with effort. Baby punches me in victory, gives my ribs a jubilant header. She seems to like it up there, it's true.

In the morning, imprints of the doctor's hands appear on my skin: curves, smudges in purple, green, yellow, imprints of a struggle.

*

When I see a woman pushing a buggy with a sling attached to her, or a buggy with a buggy board, a double buggy, a triple cinnamon buggy with foam, I wonder.

Is she relaxing into the straw of it all, the barnyard scents of multiple reproduction? Is she finding that her mind is splintering, or maybe it swirls from thing to thing, from child to child like a noble sprite.

I know multiple women who say that they have chosen their lot, and they are greatly pleased with it. This seems to be the key: to choose, and to stick with it.

The only way you will survive, someone once told me, *is to commit fully. Imagine you are in the military. Your task: to get through the day with everyone alive*.

The toddler runs out in front of a car, and I am seconds from failing in my task. I am a poor soldier, clearly, the type who would be made to run on the spot.

Afterwards I stare at the blank page for an entire morning. I feel the hours entering and leaving my body. It seems that I may never write again.

*

My best friend has her baby; to us, it happens easily, naturally, the sun rising, a new person in the world. *Forty hours of pain*, she whispers in my ear. *That'll be our band name*, I tell her. Our band of mothers, me on the triangle, her playing the xylophone using only her new, finger-solid nipples.

I speak to her husband in the kitchen. He seems to be balder than the last time I saw him. *We're really grown ups now,* he tells me. *It's finally happened.* Is this what it takes? We imagine the rule book: *stewardship of exactly three mortal souls.*

*

I am testing out a theory that I must wait for the right words, actively. They will surely appear, as the birds do to Cinderella, helpful cheerful sounds lifting the covers off my bed, singing in trees.

You will know it when you see it, my mentor tells me, over chips covered in mayonnaise. Lately we have been indulging ourselves together, as though to prove that the mind does not eat clean.

Look: the mind loves sips of beer, and kebabs eaten from sticky wobbling wooden tables. The mind still loves cigarettes, after all. In lieu of inhalation, I tap them with my fingers. I insert one, experimentally, into my ear.

You will know it when you see it, she says, taking a drag. But she is forgetting, nicely. She is forgetting that she spotted the first one. She knew what it was.

*

One day I sit down and I am writing again. It seems important not to notice that it is happening. Not to notice the ways my mind falls on the words, the way I can become – for whole seconds, or hours – the movement of a line.

Once I have written, this seems to be the important part. The words, left to grow on the page. I have surfed a wave, I like to imagine. I have ridden a horse. I am a profoundly un-sporty person, and here is the evidence.

*

The second baby will be lifted out of you, they say, and I think, how pleasant. I select some classical music for the occasion. I understand that my husband will be wearing a small, pink hat.

*

One night I show my husband the scraps I have. I throw pieces of the new book at him like birds, hoping the throwing will give them flight.

Because isn't this what you have to do to baby birds: lift them from a high window, like a turret, and let them fall to the ground. And just before they dip into the moat their wings will remember themselves, and start to move.

But so far they are only beginnings, these scraps, and they are not learning to fly. I am incubating them in a kind of zoo, let's say. They have cages up there in the turret, and there is a general smell of litter. A general smell of life: halted, held, trapped.

*

The physiotherapist has a face that is constantly tilted by pity. She asks me to list all my activities. There are only two: writing, and toddler. *Laptops are bad for your back*, she says. *Can you use a pen?*

I have seen Virginia Woolf's longhand manuscripts. I have seen the way that often, she wrote out a whole page and didn't make a single correction.

*

I try writing by hand, and it reminds me of keeping a diary aged fourteen. This is either a good or a bad thing. I was in love with Harry Taylor – my ninth love – and every time I wrote his name I drew a heart around it.

I wonder whether this work is more *authentically me*, having come entirely from my own hands, these small, yellowish, plump hands that I have always had.

I wonder whether the baby will have my hands, if she is lucky. The God books say she is being *knitted* inside me, formed by two invisible needles, pointing from heaven.

I am four, not three, the toddler pronounces seriously. *I lived in your belly for a year.*

*

Would you tell your husband to be happy that you have a new lover? my best friend asks me, months too late. (She means this: you cannot expect your first child to be happy about your second.)

But we have already broken the extremely good news to him, with cake and huge smiles. We even thought about a clown. *But clowns are terrifying*, my best friend says. *Clowns are the epitome of what you are doing: telling him to smile in the face of hell.*

But isn't that a good lesson for life anyway, I say glibly. He smiled in the face of hell. Worthy of any tombstone.

Anyway, I have never liked tedious authority, and this is what parenthood mostly consists of, so far: being told what to do.

*

At a rainy children's party in the park all the parents are forced together under a small marquee. One woman is very excitable. I think I recognise her symptoms as pre-depressive mania, the kind that sees you crafting your own Christmas presents, but I could be very wrong.

When will you have another child? she asks the host of the party. *Are you having another child? Well, we are trying*, says the host. *But it's not happening so far. I keep losing the babies.*

The host has told me that doctors and nurses keep accusing her of losing the last baby down the toilet, or in her bed. Shedding the baby without noticing anything at all. But she swears this hasn't happened, and they swear that her uterus is empty.

We imagine the child, grown gills and flippers, swimming through all the channels of her self.

*

I do not have a job, and the first child is at nursery (fingers crossed, daily). *Are you working on another book?* people ask me, and I say *yes, yes, I am. How's it going?* they ask, and I say *well. It is going well.*

My cloud storage runs out of space. It has no images, no videos. There are only words, and words. I have produced them: the act has been done, my eyes watching my hands from their corners. It has happened at the appointed time, my desk prepared as intricately as an altar, my fingers lifting over the keyboard, an ornament shifted one inch to the left. And it has happened in the middle of the kitchen, and in the early morning with the toddler's head heavy on my chest. *Important!* I tap out to myself. *Crucial!*

I have had to ignore the physiotherapist, and in reward for this I have words. A lot of words. *Enough to wrap around the earth fifty-three times*, we could say, or: *enough for thirty books*. Enough for a lifetime, floating up there in the cloud, never falling to earth.

*

My back is worse. And there is more, the beginning of a feeling between my legs exactly like a bruise. I cannot help thinking of the long debate in an undergraduate seminar about why I was more unnerved by Beckett's *kick in the cunt* than my male classmate.

Why do you hate it? he kept asking. Because some day, I should have said, I will experience this sensation fifty-four times a day.

In the course, *A410: Twentieth-Century Literature*, there was exactly one woman. In the twenty-first century, we studied this one woman as much as we could. We tried to see where she could lead us.

*

Most weeks I start a second book, and then leave it by the side of the road, pale, thin, vulnerable.

Before I ever had children I dreamt of leaving them everywhere, of course: on trains, in shopping centres, in the attic for years.

When I was younger, I was constantly having scares. During a particularly challenging essay I liked to sink to the carpet of my room, checking for blue-tinted labia. Every month, I swore that my areolas were darker, that a *Linea Nigra* was already beginning to form under my belly button. The pregnancy line.

When I went to bed, I ran names over and over for comfort: Virginia, Zora, Jean, Marianne, Grace, Charlotte. I read from the spines on my bookshelves, hoped to pass something on.

*

We know exactly when the baby will be born. And she will grow whatever I do. She will grow upside down, perhaps, but she will make her own fingers and liver and tiny pea-brain.

When I dreamed of pregnancy as a student, perhaps this is what I wished for: for it all to be taken out of my hands. For miraculous things to be done without me.

She will be born on a bank holiday. I think this is a bad sign, but I try not to. After all, my first child was born on Friday the 13th. The midwife disapproved when I made a joke about this. But there was so much blood, and gore.

*

One story: writers disappear between books. If we were to look for them in those years, we would find them wandering, translucent, people without form.

In their homes, we would find pages everywhere, sticking out of closed drawers like discarded feathers, piled in hallways, used as wallpaper, covering every surface.

Whenever they heard the word *silence*, they would laugh hysterically.

*

I have not disappeared, yet. I am seen, often. I speak and speak and speak, until I barely know my own voice. In its place, there are other women. An articulate woman on one day, a fumbling woman on the next. All of them describing something long finished, old hand-moves they tried not to see.

*

Elephants are pregnant for two years, we all know. And somewhere in the record books surely we can find a woman who was pregnant forever.

We all feel we will be pregnant forever, in fact, if we do not have a form on which we have signed our name. Yes, I have agreed, you can lift the baby out of me on 10 August. It will not be your fault if you leave me bladder-less, or bowel-less, or dead.

*

I decide to cut and paste every single thing I have written into one long Word document. I trawl through it, a child with a net on the beach, lifting the grid to the sun, looking for the flipping, silver bodies of shrimp.

Occasionally I see something alive, held on the end of my gaze, glittering. I put it away for safekeeping, in the folder on my desktop labelled *shrimp*.

*

We have bought the first child a fire engine to make up for the second. Sorry, we practise, pressing the little button on its roof to make it flash. There is no off button: you just have to wait for it to stop flashing.

You just have to wait? my husband asks, turning the fire engine over. *That doesn't seem right.*

We put the fire engine away: it will be presented on D-day, which is drawing ever closer, like a fog. When it's around us, we'll no longer be able to see it.

*

When I was waiting for my first child to be born I lay in the bath for hours. It was a downstairs bathroom at the back of the house; it had a small radiator and a flat roof and it was November.

I listened to Hildegard de Bingen and felt my soul hovering at the very edge of the abyss. I was an unexploded bomb, a star on the brink of going nuclear. I could not bear it.

*

On the scheduled day we get up early, as though for a flight or an exam. The bag has been packed weeks ago, many many sleepsuits in bundles, even though we are expected to leave the next day.

The real meaning of these many many sleepsuits is in fact a terrible illness of the child, or the mother, or time-travel back to the blessed days when they kept you in hospital for weeks. But no-one says this. They only say: pack ten sleepsuits. My bag is bulging with them, and with clothes for me, and slippers and name lists and soft cloths to drape around my breasts.

There are none of the optimistic things I packed for the first child: essential oils and whale music and meditation CDs. I had read books about women high on acid or life leaning on handsome men with long beards in California in the sixties. I was hoping for more.

But this time I am going in for surgery. I need mainly to remember to remove my jewellery, to tie back my hair, not to bleed out on the table.

*

A few days before the surgery the stargazer stops moving. She has been so active, twisting and turning, trying valiantly to get her head to point to earth.

Shine a torch up there, someone suggests. *She will follow the light.*

But on that night she is just a floating thing. She doesn't push her head to my hand like a kitten. And we go to the neon squares of the night hospital, into empty rooms where they scan me and say: it is okay. We think she is probably okay.

*

People do not talk about this: how frightening it is for the child to be invisible to you. For the child to move at will, to loop the cord around their neck, if you are very unlucky. To die, silently, without witness, right there inside your body.

*

On the last night, I dream I am at the centre of the earth. Dreams are boring to read about but: the earth is my stomach, and there are layers and layers to go through until I reach the surface. Does the womb feel like a prison, I have to wonder. Or is it more like this: a rare destination, Jules Verne discovering the core glows cold after all.

*

The atmosphere in the operating theatre is so much like a church. Everyone has their heads bowed. Everything is muffled and earnest and filled with light.

I am doing well on the morphine. I understand what the talk was about now: the talk about morphine and the talk about life.

Here is the green paper screen, the colour of the underside of a leaf, shading my opened body. Here is my husband's hand, crushed, the blood pushed away. It is white and gummy; it is rubber milk. I almost bite.

There is a kind man by my head: he twiddles dials, letting ecstasy trickle into my spine.

There is a less kind man by my stomach; he is teaching his student how to slice me accurately. They have their heads together. They are trying their best.

*

Perhaps I should not be greedy. Not a single woman in my family has ever even written one book before.

It still seems like an accident, a natural event, an act of divine intervention.

Most women writers in the past didn't even have one child, let alone two.

*

Don't look at the reflections in the lights, I read online. Don't glimpse the mess of yourself. But I do look, seeing redness, plastic fingers, mystery.

It will feel like they are doing the washing up in your stomach, someone said, as though this was a familiar sensation. In fact, it doesn't feel like anything.

I keep asking for updates, for information on the progress of their hands through my organs. But the less kind man only laughs. He doubts that I want this information.

The kind man asks if they should lower the screen, and when I say *yesyes* they scrunch it down like it is nothing, and here: she is held above my face.

I recognise her immediately, from long ago or far into the future, the arc of her cheek, the sound bell of her nose. I had been waiting for this nose. It was completely missing from my life.

But. She is blurred, purpling: her head falls forward like a painting of war. Something is wrong. They have taken her away.

Bring her, I tell them, commanding as a queen, my abdomen still an open cavity, the screen replaced now, leaned over by heads dipping, rising.

Bring her, I say, with all my breath, my mouth scream-wide, the room quiet as a dream.

*

There are more important things than books, my grandmother said to me once.

Her mother was a suffragette who set a department store on fire and leapt across the burning roofs. Then she divorced her husband – unheard of in those times – and lay around in her dressing gown all day reading.

When my grandmother came home from school nothing had been done. *Nothing!* my grandmother told me, her voice shaking with disgust.

*

On the third day or in the third hour we are told we can see her. She is alive, they tell us.

But when we see her it seems to me she has died, and it is only the tubes that are making her skin pink, and her hair fresh and shiny. Or maybe it is shining from my blood, which I can see in small, irregular scabs around her ears.

We can touch her finger through a hole in the glass box. We can watch her stomach move up and down with her breath. *Is that what breath always looks like?* I ask my husband. So much like a bagpipe, or a pulsing jellyfish, something round and fleshy, emptying and filling with air.

*

The first child comes to visit my single bed. Somewhere in my bag there is the fire engine, but when we give it to him he only looks confused and asks: *baby?*

*

At a certain point someone discovered that it was good for premature and sickly babies to be held, once they are solid enough. That a mother or father's arms can be as good as an incubator. Better.

They call it kangaroo care, of course, and we hold her in the pouch of ourselves. I joke that my husband's chest is better than mine because it is hairy. I joke.

I try to keep her tied to me until they put her back. Or until they wake me up, with some force, and tell me that I need to leave.

Downstairs in the hospital bed they put the sides up to stop me tumbling out. It is true that I have been restless in my sleep, flailing even, trying to get somewhere I don't understand.

My missing of her is sweet and viscous, like syrup. When the other babies cry, my breasts swell and leak: I am ashamed that they can't tell the difference.

*

One morning I sit up and cough, and my stomach rips open.

My guts are about to slip from me, it seems. They will roll into the bedding and I will stare at them, perfectly alert, a chicken running with no head.

They come and peel back my bandage and reassure me, soothe me after the nightmare. It was just a dream, they say, or words to this effect. Your stomach is intact.

I think of the old smoothness of my belly above my jeans, the way it flattened into the denim. I thought I wanted someone else to touch it, but nothing was better than holding it myself, cupping the sloping skin in my palm.

*

She opens her eyes and gives us curious little looks, as though wondering why we have put her through all of this.

Why did you bother, we ventriloquise, doing a silly voice. We stop. Her voice would sound nothing like that.

She looks like she is approximately 300 years old. Like she has appraised the whole world, the whole universe, and found it distinctly lacking.

*

I will write another book, I decide, on a darkening summer evening in the hospital, when she has been allowed to fall asleep on my chest. *I will really do it this time*, I tell her. She holds my hand with her own, squeezes, holds tight.

The world outside is honey-lit: it is endless. In the trees the birds are making their homes. Swarms of insects are living their three-day lives. The cars roar on.

I whisper these words to her. I tell her all about it.

FENG LI

I

XXIV

II

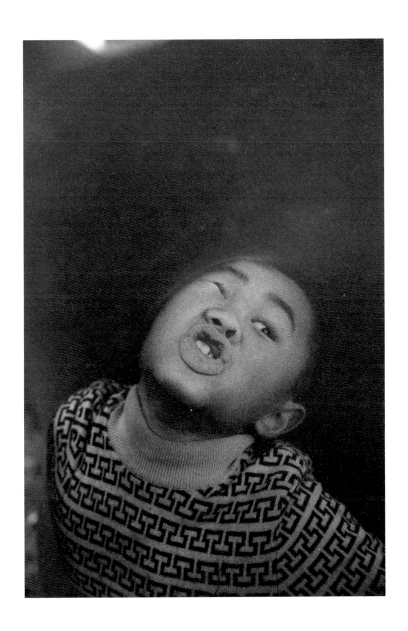

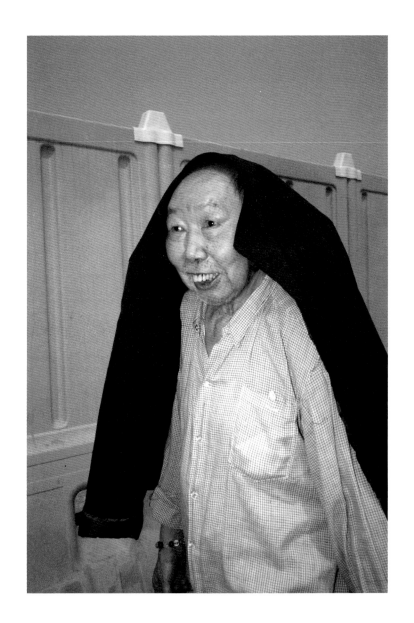

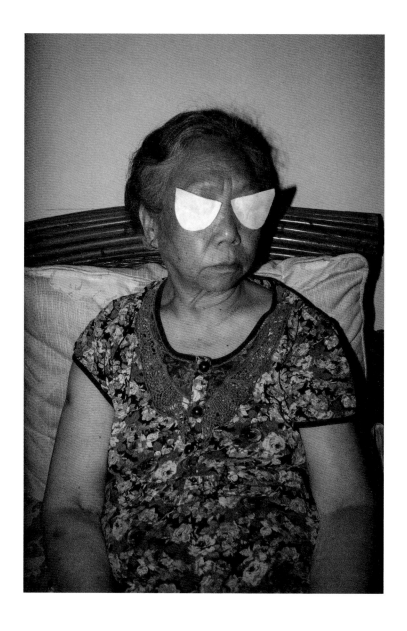

KATE POTTS

POETRY

ANIMAL SONG (II)

'The rarer they get, the fewer meanings animals can
have. Eventually rarity is all they are made of.'
Helen Macdonald, *H is for Hawk*

I shuffle my sitbones back   neck craned
like a turtle's towards   the dashboard

where my fingernails
          flutter a rainpulse.   I scan
   the windowscreen horizon, scan my eye-
corners for
     a breath-catch twitch, a familiar startle:

rabbitfur, gullwing, pheasant russet or
     crest – ear – escaping rear – the
fractured
animal parts we still glimpsed (though
a rarity) when we were kids;

these days we encounter those same beasts
in glassy hallucination, wishful
        mindtricks   or soupy, in dreams.

Those bodies of bone/ fur/ flesh/ were,
together, our compass   their chitter
and call   a conglomerate pattern
of sound we set, and knew, our song by. Not

this blankened land, no other mind for miles.

Lunchtimes we spill/ stalk down from
     our concrete warrens, eat paper cupfuls
     of mossy, green-specked chaw.
The advertisements
          promise *pureorganicnatural.*

Reader
     careful, careful   were you to reach
your fingers to my skin, then carve
  on through, press in – blade beneath my
breastbone (past the toothsuck, hurt)
  you'd find,
in the cool cave of my ribs,   this bloodied
       bird   my heart
is singing.

SCANDEROON
[scan-der *oon*]

n

A leather drinking pouch suspended from a cavalry officer's belt. 1863: *If a man may rest, he might quaff the dregs of his scanderoon.*

Or, scanderoon: a rainy day stash: If a woman may finally rest, she might break out her put-by scanderoon. She might eat up every last salted crumb and hike off into her sleep

    the hills demarcating – finding focus
        as we taxi down from altitude; the canopy's densening, seabed green.

Or, scanderoon: a homing pigeon, supposedly of Persian origin, of a breed having long heads, bodies, and legs, broad shoulders, and a long iron-clad compass bill with moderate wattle. A slick, swerving bird.

Or, the message a pigeon carries around its neck through thousands of miles – in war, or peacetime. Untraceable, off-web, hidden up there inside fat cloud or behind a brush of sun.

Or scanderoon (hist): in Rev James Stromingam's Whitby Glossary, 1791: 'Scanderoon: a popular mis-quote; a sentence or phrase wrongly apportioned'.

For instance, I never called my dictionary 'prison';
I never doused it in bleach or buried it, never said 'If I can't dance, it's not my dictionary'.

When all the rivers are breached and the lodestars dark;
when the sea re-hems the map
and your bones are long gone cold;

when the right word is as rare
as a snowbird in hell – I'll still be circling in,
trusting my magnet-beak, striking for home.

PISTONS AND BONES

I remember my mother explaining very practically
how she thought shock therapy worked:
electric current recalibrating the skewed chemistry of the brain.
I sat in the back garden and imagined electrons like vitamin C powder
in a sphere of water, fizzing into an orange flush.

   In one of the photographs, my grandfather's skin is pillowy and buoyant.
   He is twelve years old, gaze turned inwards, standing next to his brothers
   who are stiff in their well-worn army uniforms.
   In the other photograph, he is herculean and broad-chested –

His suit struggles to contain him; my mother is getting married.

   He was never got right by the old regimes, He was never
   got right by the shared clothes, the Gideon bible.
   Most visitors regarded him, he said, the way a cow would look at you.

On a bad day, my mother said, her father would calmly announce after dinner
that he was going to stand in the road and wait for something to run him over.

On a bad day, she said, he would bolt out of the house and away,
taking his clothes off as he went, leaving little fabric puddles in his wake.
His children would run out, scooping up those familiar garments and forging
      on after him.

   On a bad day, my mother said, he would bolt out of the house and away.

Was it freedom, to loose himself first from his house and then
from his jacket, shirt and shoes, sloughing himself out of his everyday life?

   I have sometimes imagined him keeping going,
   peeling off his pale, broad, Nottingham skin to dump it lightly in the gutter.

      And then the knots of his muscles;
      and then the twiggish veins, his pistons and bones.
      And then his pulse – the ghost of all this momentum – hovering inert
      like a jellyfish, before expiring into the Tuesday morning air.

LULLABY GIRL
After Eileen McAuley's *The Seduction*

flourbaby   doughbaby   squaresack   canvas
sewingmachinestitched   moonface/ no face
dumpy/ dinted   the sack sits tight   sweaty
against your poly-cotton   thin white shirt
chubby squat   school tie   long tail tucked in
against your chest

this is what
    it's like: heavysack   sleeps in a cardboard
box   under your bed   think back
to your doll   dad in the Argos queue
you wanted   water sloshed in its pink   belly
squeezed from between its pink legs   shaken
from blue   painted-on eyes   hinged lids   not
2lb flour bag in your skinny arms   you sing
hush hush in your head at the bus stop,   corner
shop

            could not bring yourself to look
last year   at Charlie Ward's newborn   pudgy
clay   animal   rumpled eyes   still
oblivious   in the pram though your classmates
crowded over its sky   made the right *oooo*
sound   in your head it was   animated   doll

you're still slight   gristle-breasted   nowhere
near woman   Miss Juegos said   *ask yourself:*
what care is needed by the flourbaby?   who is
with the flourbaby?   where is the flourbaby?
snug in the bottom drawer, under
your magazines   *if there were boys at school*
you'd all be at it nonstop   Miss Mcclure says

limbsjumble/ snog spittle open
mouth never learning all   hunger and dumb-
ness
                    Sian disappears takes her tight
belly   oval   swells   with her   Mr Wojcik
sings   *Too Much Too Young*   over and over
you hear   Kelly, before her trial   is trying
for a baby
                easy,   easy,   baby   a beautiful
shackle, or, like a ticket out   of somewhere,
maybe   rope ladder to cling to dig
fingernails in   something   *mine*   hot hot
shame and shameless/ bigbodied I   *made* this

in the first poem   you've studied in years
it's called *despicable*   this girl/mother-
hood state   called *feminine*   *void*

JOAN JONAS   INTERVIEW

'I didn't see a major difference between a poem, a sculpture, a film, or a dance. A gesture has for me the same weight as a drawing: draw, erase, draw, erase – memory erased.'   Joan Jonas, 1983

For over five decades, Joan Jonas's work has demonstrated a disciplinary elasticity rare in contemporary art: through her performances (often involving her own presence, alone or in the company of others), drawings (many of animals), sculptures (often with abstract, geometric references), environments and video installations (which comprise all the above, and include objects, props and complex display systems). Jonas's work is rich in literary reference, from Halldór Laxness's novels to scientific manuals, from Hilda Doolittle's poetry to Aby Warburg's essays. Her elliptical, fluid and non-narrative time-based pieces – performances, lecture performances, films and videos – seem to suggest that time isn't linear, that there are many ways to tell a story, and that space can be constantly altered. In parallel, a growing environmental consciousness in her recent work – and an ongoing collaboration with her pet dogs – has cemented her position as a fundamental voice in our present times of ecological unrest.

In a moment in which artistic creation seems to be moving away from the demands of knowledge-production towards a less didactic, more personal relationship to understanding, Joan Jonas's art has gained its current well-deserved attention. This rise of interest in her practice has coincided with a series of important monographic institutional exhibitions, including *Light Time Tales* (2014–15) at HangarBicocca, Milan, which in many ways anticipated *They Come to Us Without a Word* (2015), her large-scale project for the United States Pavilion at the 56th Venice Biennale. In 2017, *What is Found in the Windowless House is True* at Gavin Brown's Enterprise became her largest solo show in New York since *Five Works*, an exhibition held at the Queens Museum of Art in the winter of 2003–4. 2018 will see major survey shows, co-organised by the Tate Modern, London, and Haus der Kunst, Munich, and also held at the Serralves Foundation in Porto later in the year.

This conversation took place in early January in Portland, Jamaica, at the Alligator Head Foundation, an organisation dedicated to the area's marine preservation initiated by TBA-21, whose Academy has commissioned a new work from Jonas. The artist's stay there coincided with its development, which largely focused on marine and local cultures and endangered habitats. Our dialogue took this new work as a starting point from which to reflect on her practice, her relationship to source materials and motifs, and to our present times. FILIPA RAMOS

TWR   How did this new commission come into being: what were its references, its starting point?
JJ   There were actually several different threads that came together in Venice for *They Come to Us Without a Word* [Jonas's presentation at the 2015 Venice Biennale]. But it started in 2010, when I began to work with Halldór Laxness's novel *Under the Glacier* for a part of *Reanimation* [a performance combining choreography, drawings and closed-circuit video projections, accompanied by music]. I called it a lecture-performance, but it was really a performance for the camera witnessed by the audience. And it's now part of the final version of *Reanimation*, the installation. It's based on actions I do with my hands and with photographs and special effects, made in my studio. I was really interested in the very poetic way in which Laxness writes about nature. I think what he says is beautiful. For instance, the way he describes what the bee does, that it's a super communion. A miracle. And that influenced, at that moment, how I began to think about certain creatures and the phenomenon of what they can do, which is kind of miraculous. At the same time, I had to consider the fact that *Under the Glacier* was written in the 1960s, while now the glaciers are melting, therefore the piece became partly focused on the situation of the environment and what's going on in relation to the climate, the creatures and the land. Then, at about the same time I had a project in Japan [*They Come to Us Without a Word*, CCA Kitakyushu Project Gallery, Kitakyushu, 2013], which was not related to Laxness's book. On my

way to Japan I was thinking of all the fish the Japanese eat, and I decided to make 100 drawings of fish. This group of drawings was presented in Japan and no place else, though I included them in a different way in my show in Venice. *Reanimation*, on the other hand, had already been fully developed and realised as a performance and an installation. I continued to be inspired by Laxness, even if I wasn't focused on him. That statement about bees became part of the Venice installation. I had five different rooms in Venice: bees, fish, mirror, wind and homeroom. The bees specifically related to him. Later, I was invited by Francesca von Habsburg and Markus Reymann to do a performance about the oceans. I first presented it as a lecture performance, which is a kind of new form for me, and I called it *Oceans - Sketches and Notes*. It became a parallel, ongoing project that I haven't finished, and it's not even fully developed. But I began this work by going back to what I did in Venice with fish. I will continue to work on the performance, but in the end it will also take the form of an installation. By now I've collected too much material to include in just a performance.

TWR   I'm interested in the presence of fish and of fishing – as well as other sea creatures, mermaids for instance – in your work. Going back to the series of fish drawings that you made for the exhibition in Japan, and also thinking about your animal drawings in general, did they come from your own imagination, or are they based on books?
JJ   No, they were copies. I mean, I made those

drawings by copying them from a book, which is the way I work. I found an old book about Japanese fish in a second-hand bookstore in San Diego – a beautiful book, with illustrations, beautiful drawings. It's purely information, a nature encyclopaedia from Japan. I made those drawings by opening up the book and choosing a certain fish to copy. I'd put it on the ground and then I'd copy it as an ink drawing with blue ink on paper, very fast. So they're not exact copies, but they're totally based on those particular fish. I include all different kinds of fish. I'll say that in general I never make up my own animals, I'd rather go directly from nature.

TWR These marine creatures seems to have a growing presence in your more recent work. Is there a growth of an environmental consciousness in present times that's permeating your practice and shaping your understanding of the sea?
JJ I've always been interested in the world of so-called nature. This is just something that we're all thinking about now, but which has come into focus in my work over the last ten years. Besides fish, I've also been drawing birds for the past few years. A friend gave me a book about birds in Thailand, and so I began to copy those. Before embarking on this oceans project, I was beginning to develop a project about birds and trees, which I'll take up again at some point.

I recall that Ute Meta Bauer told me something really interesting: she said that in the Pacific, people don't believe that there's a separation between the sea and the land, but that they are one and the same

thing. So birds aren't exactly a different subject from fish. And I wish I could somehow incorporate that assumption into this project, because it combines these two interests of mine. But no, I've always been interested in nature. I love to work in different landscapes and to deal with their inherent situations. But the only animal I've really worked with is the dog, with my own dogs.

TWR This year you're going to have a big retrospective exhibition, which opens in March at the Tate Modern. You can do a retrospective in many ways; how has this show has been conceived? What are the specific threads, choices and ideas behind it?
JJ I call it a survey show because it's not really a big retrospective. It's a limited number of pieces. In particular, it's a development from a larger show at the HangarBicocca in Milan, *Light Time Tales* [an exhibition of installations and single-channel videos ranging from across Jonas's career, 2014]. There I just made a selection of as many as possible of my favourite pieces. There were some works that I couldn't show due to the environmental situation of the space. Andrea Lissoni, the exhibition's curator, collaborated with me, of course; he'll also be the curator for the show at the Tate. In the past I've always wanted to control exactly what I show, with the help of a curator, but in this case, I enjoy Andrea's input into the process. Naturally there are threads that go through my work, but the show will not follow a specific theme or chronology. *The Juniper Tree* [1976, turned into an installation in 1994] is owned by the Tate, so that will be

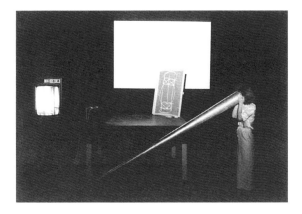

included, partly because it was my first narrative fairy tale. I've wanted to show the *Organic Honey* series [Jonas's first performance to integrate video, 1972] since Milan. For me it is really important to have that piece; we can't show it at the Tate because there's no room for it, but we'll show it in Munich and in Portugal. I wanted to do an outdoor piece based on my early outdoor works, and Catherine Wood, another curator, came up with the idea of doing it on the Thames. It's sort of a gamble. We're also going to show something called *Stage Sets*. This was totally Andrea's idea – I never would have thought of that. But he really insisted on it, and I think for a good reason.

TWR　Can you tell us a bit more about *Stage Sets*? Is it a display or a proper artwork?
JJ　It was a work that I made for an exhibition (*Joan Jonas/Stage Sets*) at the Institute of Contemporary Art of the University of Pennsylvania in 1977. It's a combination of props and elements from different stage sets of the 1970s: receding paper walls from *Funnel*, a six-foot metal hoop, a group of accounting chairs from *Organic Honey*, tin cones from *Mirage* hanging from the ceiling as light fixtures, an octagonal structure like a magic mirror box, a table with a drawing on it against a wall with another drawing on that – all arranged in a certain way to suggest a stage set. This work does not include video, so it's rather different in nature from the other works in the show. It's more sculptural.

TWR　Despite the fact that you seemed to have

left behind more conventional approaches to sculpture at an early phase of your career, there continues to be a strong sense of volume and a specific construction of space within your work. Do you see this interest as an ongoing dialogue with the tradition of sculpture?
JJ　Yes. From the time when I stepped from sculpture to performance, I thought of bringing my ideas about sculptural space to my performances. I've always made 'stage sets', so the transition to installation was a natural one. I really do consider this a kind of expanded sculpture. It's interesting that, in academic institutions, the kind of work that I do was first accepted by sculpture departments.

TWR　I'd like to move to your performing activity, to your performing self, when you sometimes become a blackbird, as in *Merlo* (1974), a howling dog (*Waltz*, 2003), a seducing woman (*Organic Honey*). Do you see these gestures as a way to becoming other?
JJ　I don't think of it exactly that way. From the very beginning I was role-playing. I thought of performing as playing roles. So after the *Mirror* pieces [a series of performance and video works begun in the 1960s], which were very abstract and not at all about representing a character or anything, I began to work with characters, starting from *Organic Honey*. Organic Honey is a character that I created with masks and costumes – a female persona that was androgynous also, and I shifted back and forth in the piece in these disguises. And from that time on and until recently, I really focused on playing

roles of women. In *Lines in the Sand* I was interested in the poet H. D., Hilda Doolittle, who wrote *Helen in Egypt*, a version of the Trojan War with Helen of Troy as its main character. I didn't want to play H. D. or Helen, but their personas and their presence inspired the subject matter of the work. While I didn't directly represent them, there were many references. So it's always about disguises and role-play. When I begin to work on a performance, I always try to imagine who or what I represent, and I often just find a costume – a dress, a hat – to give me an identity. It's not easy to talk about or describe what happens when I enter into the performative aspect, when it becomes non-verbal, and I am interacting with the material and moving, trying to find movement. Over the years I've worked with movement in several different ways. Lately, not focusing on tasks.

TWR   What about in the performance *The Shape, the Scent, the Feel of Things* (2004), which responds to the life and work of Aby Warburg? What was your relation to Warburg there?
JJ   I never became Aby Warburg. But I did speak his text. In that piece I play the parts with Ragani Haas, who was the other woman performing. José Luis Blondet played Aby Warburg, because I wanted the character to really have dimension. That was very conscious. That had to be played by another performer. And Ragani and I were different, we were the nurses in the sanatorium. I thought of that space at Dia:Beacon as being the sanatorium where Warburg was living when he wrote that text [*Images

from the Region of the Pueblo Indians of North America*] about the Hopi people. The performance took place in the basement of Dia:Beacon in a long narrow corridor defined by columns with the audience sitting on a bleacher at one end. There were very high ceilings. Then I entered into another kind of performative dimension, while not playing any particular person. Just pure performance. And there's a voiceover in which I'm reciting his words and the titles of photographs. Because I didn't want to use any of his images that he took in the Southwest. So while I represent Warburg, I'm not playing Warburg at all.

TWR   You've been working as an artist for an extended period of time. How has age and ageing influenced your performing?
JJ   I can't do strenuous things the way I used to, but so far it hasn't hampered me. I'm not interested in exerting myself in a certain way any more. There's a limit to what I can do, jumping up and down and running around, for instance. But that's why I'm working on another kind of movement. For my piece *Stream or River, Flight or Pattern* [a multimedia installation exploring the relations between humans and the environment, 2016-2017], I was interested in developing another kind of movement for myself, in the work. I perform in the projections, in costumes, and in this place I'm not playing a particular role. I'm not representing a particular character. I'm moving in relation to the projected background, as I consider the visual effects of this interaction. The movements are

really choreographed, and partly determined by this shallow space that I have to work in, in order to remain fully in the projection. I'm continuing to work this way in this new piece, commissioned by TBA21. I'm interested in the form of a lecture-demonstration, which in this case is about articulating information and a longer-than-usual verbal narrative, in relation to pure movement and performance, as I interact with the projected video images. And the subjects that I'm dealing with – the sea, sea creatures, mermaids, and so on. Mermaids exist in this work because I decided, as I always do, to deal with myth.

TWR   I'm particularly curious about your collaboration with dogs.
JJ   I've had three dogs in my adult life. The first was Sappho, and I always say that Sappho was a saint; Zina was a comedian. I'm not sure about Ozu. He's sort of a prince. Sappho... She is in my work, and you see her, she's more of a person. She's a very beautiful dog, with one blue eye and one brown eye. The image of the dog is all through my work. And also the image of that dog, of each dog I've had and I've drawn.
    In *Organic Honey*, for instance, I was exploring from the very beginning the function of myth. So one idea is the concept of the animal helper that women have. An animal helper can be a cat or a horse. The force that drives you, the animal force, energy. So, in *Organic Honey*, I justify the idea of having a dog as being the animal helper, a driving force... and then I become a dog and I howl. I was

slightly influenced by Djuna Barnes's *Nightwood* (1936), where Nora, one of the female characters, howls like a dog. Then Zina, the second dog. I drew her over and over again, I was fascinated with her. She was the one who decided to enter into my work. Every time I got up to make something in front of the camera she'd get into it, because she'd come and interact with me. I never told her what to do. She just participated.

TWR   Was she the one jumping the hoop in one of the *My New Theater* pieces?
JJ   Yes, well, I did tell her to jump in the hoop. I taught her so she could easily do it. I think Sappho could jump through a hoop too, but Ozu won't go near it. I recently made a piece called *Beautiful Dog* (2014), with Ozu in it. We tied a GoPro camera onto his collar. It recorded upside down facing backwards through his back legs. He's very different to those two dogs. They're cattle dogs, shepherds, and they have a different way of relating to people or to a situation. Ozu is a poodle, and I haven't yet made many drawings of him. So I want to do more with Ozu but it's a different process – he is very sensitive, very intelligent, but he'll behave in his own way. He is intent on trying to understand what I'm saying when I speak to him. He understands many words.

TWR   My favourite work of yours is *Barking* (1972). The reason I like it so much is that it takes the interest some of your earlier works have in distance and perception, and turns it to a more

intimate sort of triangle between a camera, an
animal and two women. In the black-and-white
video, you can't see what the dog is doing, but she's
barking and there's a person following her, plus
the camera. I like how the triangular relationship
between person, machine and dog is so articulated
in such a simple video. And I was curious to know
how it came into being.

JJ   Oh, that's funny. Well, that video was shot in
Nova Scotia in 1972. Actually Simone [Forti] was
visiting me. And from the very beginning when
I started going to Nova Scotia, I had my camera
and I recorded everyday events, choreographed
actions, and the landscape. I really love the landscape there. So, my camera was at hand. It was
recorded in the kitchen of an old house. And the
dog was outside, and it was barking. So I picked
up the camera and started to record it, and Simone
walked into the room and said 'She's still barking.'
It was just something that came together in a very
organic way. I haven't looked at it in a long time,
I should look at it. But it's just organic, the way
things in my life happen. The unplanned becomes
part of my work.

F. R.,
January 2018

Joan Jonas at Tate Modern, 14 March–5 August
2018 and *BMW Tate Live Exhibition 2018: Ten Days
Six Nights* at Tate Modern, 16–25 March 2018.

The topics approached in the introduction unfolded
in the text 'The Animal Company She Keeps: Joan
Jonas's Multispecies Collaboration', part of *Place.
Labour. Capital* (NTU Centre for Contemporary
Art, 2017). Thank you to the book's editor Anca
Rujoiu for her valuable contribution to my thinking
about Joan Jonas's practice.

LOST LUNAR APOGEE
DANIELLE DUTTON

At dinner a poet visiting from China said he planned, the following day, to try to get inside T. S. Eliot's childhood home. Someone else at the table, another man from China but who'd lived in St Louis for years, told a story about being shown into the very house when he and his wife had been looking to buy. He hadn't realised where he was until he was inside it. He saw stairs for the family and stairs for the servants. 'They wanted everything separate,' he said. I knew only one person at the table. Like most of the others, she was a poet. It was cold in the cellar of the restaurant where we'd all met to celebrate the Chinese poet's visit, and out of three small square windows, high up in the whitewashed wall, were plants shaped like coral but bright green. 'It must have been a lot of work,' the second man suddenly said into a bit of silence. I nodded with the others, though I had no idea what he meant. Then the waiter set down my wine. 'Lunar Apogee,' he announced. What a dippy name for a wine, I thought, as the woman to my right said it was the perfect title for a first book of poems destined to win awards. Was it the wine, then, that got us talking about Mina Loy – 'Moreover,' she wrote, 'the Moon —' – and not T. S. Eliot's boyhood home? My friend claimed she'd seen Loy's handprint on a sidewalk in Greenwich Village. Someone else said he'd visited her grave in Aspen. 'She's everywhere,' said the woman to my right, waving her arms in the air as if Mina Loy herself might at any moment appear. Did I smile or laugh? The waiter set down a plate. Whenever I think of Loy, I said, taking my turn at the silence, I think of that ethereal black-and-white photograph of her face – eyes closed, hair loose. Light breaks across her shoulder, and she turns herself into it ever so slightly. Then the Chinese poet smiled at me, and I felt strangely unnerved. I could never be so unselfconscious in a photograph, I said. 'Die in the past, live in the future!' exclaimed the woman to my right. But isn't it ridiculous, I thought – I didn't say this part out loud; the conversation moved on without me – that after all the words of hers I've read – 'The human cylinders / Revolving in the enervating dusk' – all those poems – when I think of Mina Loy I think of a pretty face? Of course thinking isn't looking, I went on, no doubt trying to justify my own superficiality, uneasy at having always been somewhat superficial in this way, but while my purest thought of Mina Loy might be an image of her face, that image is itself a kind of thought. It is Mina Loy's face beset by or in some way accountable to certain words or ideas, which, in turn, bring further images with them: Mina Loy's face and the cover of *The Lost Lunar Baedeker* (those long thermometer earrings); her drawing of a figure shaking sky out of its hair; Joseph Cornell's 'Portrait of Mina Loy' (she in a hat, smiling, atop a constellation); Mina Loy's face and those star-shaped lamps she made. It's no wonder she is celestial in my mind – ethereal, impossible. In a letter dated 3 July 1951, Cornell himself wrote to her to say: 'I had a beautiful early morning in the back yard under the Chinese quince tree – very early, in fact not much after five; and I could not help but think of you, looking up at the moon, when the first rays of the sun turn its gold into silver.' I felt sad then, suddenly forlorn, not sure why I'd spoken at all, and ridiculously middle-aged – no one had ever written me such a letter or ever would, sitting under a quince tree – sitting at that table with the handsome Chinese poet, thinking about a handprint on a sidewalk in New York. 'It was not given to each of us / To be desired,' wrote Mina Loy. I ordered a second glass of wine, a third. Now my problems were upon me, and I quietly seethed while stuffing myself with cracked Moroccan olives. The night was plainly doomed to spiral down. But an hour later, in a brightly lit gallery on Cherokee Street, the poet read his poems in Mandarin. After each, my friend read the English translation, and the poet sat to listen in the empty chair to my left. I felt a kind of intimacy with him then, though we never spoke, only smiled each time he sat, and especially near the end, side-by-side, listening to her read a poem in which a man whose wife has recently died sits alone at a table eating tangerines as inside his bookcase snow begins to fall.

On the drive home, snow began to fall. I passed an accident on Magnolia, another at McRee. It was in front of one of the old World's Fair mansions on Lindell Boulevard – the one that looks like a French chateau with wings – that under a streetlamp I saw her – 'And "Immortality" / mildews . . . / in the museums of the moon' – fur coat and gloves, snow in her long brown hair. There was no mistaking that face. I almost got into an accident myself, swerving hard to avoid a dog that streaked out from the park. My hands shook on the wheel. I had to pull over. The street was deserted. I blamed the wine, of course, cheapest on the list. I couldn't even bring myself to look in the rearview mirror. I'm driving home, I said out loud, as if to convince myself. So I did, my car at the curb, hurrying up the path – I was stamping my rubber boots on the porch when the moon broke free from the clouds, landing on the fallen snow, the street asleep and alight: 'the eye-white sky-light / white-light district.' In the Introduction to *The Lost Lunar Baedeker* we're told Loy named her book 'not for the sun but for its ghost'. Would we call the moon a ghost, or this a ghostly light? But I felt better, I did, turning my key in the lock, lucky to be home. Still, I couldn't stop shivering. Even my teeth felt cold. Here was the breakfast table strewn with the morning paper, there was my teacup, I passed through the hall – and yet I was not soothed. Everything felt off, staged. It was like walking through a photograph instead of through a home. And though it was after midnight, I swear I could hear my husband upstairs reading to our son, the story about a boy who finds a fallen star and is forced by his teacher to swallow it, then zooms into the sky. I felt a little dizzy on the landing. 'An ocean of glittering blue-black waves,' I heard my husband say, 'under a sky of huge galaxies.' I touched the bedroom door. I stepped into the light. It was my son who was the first to scream, which is how you can be sure this story is true.

JOANNA BIGGS has worked at the *London Review of Books* since 2005. She co-founded Silver Press with Sarah Shin and Alice Spawls in 2017. Her book, *All Day Long*, about modern work, came out in 2015.

VICTORIA ADUKWEI BULLEY is a British-born Ghanaian poet, writer and filmmaker. A Barbican Young Poets alumna, her work has been commissioned by the Royal Academy of Arts in addition to featuring on BBC Radio 4 *Woman's Hour*, and in *The Poetry Review*. She was shortlisted for the Brunel University African Poetry Prize 2016, and is a Complete Works Poetry fellow. Victoria's debut pamphlet, *Girl B*, edited by Kwame Dawes, forms part of the 2017 New-Generation African Poets series. She is the director of *MOTHER TONGUES*, a poetry translation and film series supported by Arts Council England and Autograph ABP, and is also co-curator of TCR Poetry, a monthly reading series based at Waterstones Tottenham Court Road.

KAYO CHINGONYI is an Anthony Burgess Fellow at The University of Manchester and poetry editor at *The White Review*. His first full-length collection of poems, *Kumukanda*, was published by Chatto & Windus in 2017.

JON DAY teaches English at King's College, London. Before this he worked as a bicycle courier in London, a job he wrote about in his first book *Cyclogeography*. He has written essays and reviews for the *London Review of Books*, *n+1*, and the *New York Review of Books*, is a regular book critic for the *Financial Times*, and a columnist for *British Homing World*, the UK's premier pigeon racing paper.

ZYGMUNT DAY is a musician and construction worker. He operates solo and with the band Echo Pressure.

AMANDA DEMARCO is a translator living in Berlin.

DANIELLE DUTTON's most recent book is the novel *Margaret the First*. In the autumn of 2018, Wave Books will reprint her novel *SPRAWL* with an afterword by Renee Gladman. Dutton is co-founder and editor of the feminist press Dorothy, a publishing project.

JOHANNA HEDVA is the author of the novel *On Hell* (Sator Press, 2018). Her fiction, essays, and poems have appeared in *Black Warrior Review*, *Entropy*, *Mask Magazine*, *3:AM*, *Triple Canopy*, and elsewhere. Her work has been shown at Machine Project, Human Resources LA, the LA Architecture and Design Museum, and the Museum of Contemporary Art on the Moon. 'Jonah' is an excerpt from her novel-in-progress *The Twin*.

MEGAN HUNTER was born in Manchester in 1984 and studied English Literature at Sussex and Cambridge. Her poetry has been shortlisted for the Bridport Prize and she was a finalist for the Aesthetica Creative Writing Award. Her first book, *The End We Start From*, was published in 2017 in the UK, US, and Canada, and has been translated into seven languages. It was shortlisted for Novel of the Year at the Books Are My Bag Readers Awards and is longlisted for the Aspen Words Prize.

ANTHONY JOSEPH is a British/ Trinidadian poet, novelist, musician and academic. His latest volume of poetry is *Rubber Orchestras* (Salt, 2011) and his latest album is entitled *Caribbean Roots*. He is a Colm Tóibín Fellow at The University of Liverpool.

SANAM KHATIBI (born 1979 in Tehran, Iran, lives and works in Brussels, Belgium) has recently had solo exhibitions at rodolphe janssen, Brussels, Belgium; The Cabin LA, Los Angeles, CA; Super Dakota, Brussels; NICC, Brussels; trampoline, Antwerp; Island, Brussels; and has participated in group shows at Various Small Fires, Los Angeles, CA; Christine König Gallery, Vienna; Museum of Deinze, Deinze and rodolphe janssen, Brussels. She will participate in an upcoming group show at MAC Marseille in the spring of 2018.

FENG LI (born 1971 in Chengdu) started taking photographs as a civil servant for the provincial Department of Communication. As an independent artist he started working on his series 'White Night' in 2005, focussing on the bizarre and the mundane in everyday

life in China. Feng Li won the 2017 Jimei ×
Arles Discovery Award.

SASCHA MACHT studied at the German
Institute for Literature. His writing has received
support from the Cultural Foundation of the
State of Saxony, and from the Senate of Berlin.
In 2015, he won the New German Fiction
contest. This is an excerpt from his first novel,
Der Krieg im Garten des Königs der Toten (The
War in the Garden of the King of the Dead),
which won the 2016 Silberschwein Prize. He
lives in Leipzig.

ELLEN DE MEUTTER (born 1981) lives and
works in Antwerp. She has had solo shows at
Tim Van Laere Gallery, Antwerp and Roberts
& Tilton, L. A.. Group shows in which she's
participated include *Secrets and Lies*, Museum of
Contemporary Art San Diego, San Diego and
Accidental Thoughts and Metaphors, Ana Cristea
Gallery, New York.

HATTY NESTOR has published in *Art In
America*, *Bomb Magazine*, *Frieze*, and many other
publications. She was Jerwood Arts Space
writer in residence 2017, and currently lives
in New Mexico. Her book on portraits of the
incarcerated is forthcoming from Zero Books
in 2019.

KATE POTTS is a poet, academic and editor.
Her second poetry collection, *Feral*, is due from
Bloodaxe in September 2018. She teaches at
Oxford University, Royal Holloway, and the
Poetry School.

MERYL PUGH has a PhD in Critical and
Creative Writing from the University of East
Anglia. The author of two pamphlets – *The
Bridle* (Salt Publishing, 2011) and *Relinquish*
(Arrowhead, 2007) – she teaches creative
writing and poetry for Morley College. Her first
collection, *Natural Phenomena*, is published in
February 2018 by
Penned in the Margins.

FILIPA RAMOS is a writer and editor based
in London, where she works as Editor in Chief
of *art-agenda*. She has a longstanding interest in
the ways artists' cinema looks at animals.

ALEV SCOTT is a journalist formerly
based in Istanbul, and the author of *Turkish
Awakening* (Faber, 2014). Her articles appear
in the *Financial Times*, *Times Literary Supplement*,
Newsweek and the *Guardian*. This piece is an
extract from *Ottoman Odyssey: Travels Through a
Lost Empire*, which will be published in October
by Quercus.

CHRIS SUCCO (born 1979) lives and works
in Düsseldorf. His work has been shown in solo
shows at the Almine Rech Gallery, London and
Brussels, Cabinet, Milan, The Journal Gallery,
LA and New York and DUVE Berlin, Berlin,
among other galleries.

PLATES

FRIENDS OF THE WHITE REVIEW

AARON BOGART
ABI MITCHELL
ABIGAIL YUE WANG
ADAM FREUDENHEIM
ADAM HALL
ADAM SAUNBY
ADELINE DE MONSEIGNAT
AGRI ISMAIL
AJ DEHANY
ALAN MURRIN
ALBA ZIEGLER-BAILEY
ALBERT BUCHARD
ALEX GREINER
ALEX MCDONALD
ALEX MCELROY
ALEXA MITTERHUBER
ALICE OSWALD
ALIX MCCAFFREY
AMBIKA SUBRAMANIAM
AMI GREKO
AMY SHERLOCK
ANASTASIA SVOBODA
ANASTASIA VIKHORNOVA
AND OTHER STORIES
ANDREW CURRAN
ANDREW LELAND
ANDREW ROADS
ANNA DELLA SUBIN
ANNA WHITE
ANNE MEADOWS
ANNE WALTON
ARCHIPELAGO BOOKS
ARIANNE LOVELACE
ARIKE OKE
ASIA LITERARY AGENCY
AUDE FOURGOUS
BAPTISTE VANPOULLE
BARBARA HORIUCHI
BARNEY WALSH
BEN HINSHAW
BEN LERNER
BEN POLLNER
BERNADETTE EASTHAM
BOOK/SHOP
BRIAN WILLIAMS
BRIGITTE HOLLWEG
BROOMBERG & CHANARIN
CAMILLE GAJEWSKI
CAMILLE HENROT
CARLOTTA EDEN
CAROL HUSTON

CAROLINE LANGLEY
CAROLINE YOUNGER
CAROLYN LEK
CARRIE ETTER
CATHERINE HAMILTON
CERI JANE WEIGHTMAN
CHARLES LUTYENS
CHARLIE HARKIN
CHARLOTTE COHEN
CHARLOTTE GRACE
CHEE LUP WAN
CHINA MIÉVILLE
CHISENHALE GALLERY
CHRIS KRAUS
CHRIS WEBB
CHRISTIAN LORENTZEN
CHRISTOPHER GRAY
CJ CAREY
CLAIRE DE DIVONNE
CLAIRE DE ROUEN
CLAIRE-LOUISE BENNETT
CLAUDE ADJIL
CODY STUART
CONOR DELAHUNTY
COSMO LANDESMAN
CRISTOBAL BIANCHI
CYNTHIA & WILLIAM
MORRISON-BELL
CYRILLE GONZALVES
DANIEL COHEN
DANIELA BECHLY
DANIELA SUN
DAVID AND HARRIET POWELL
DAVID ANDREW
DAVID BARNETT
DAVID BREUER
DAVID EASTHAM
DAVID ROSE
DAVID THORNE
DEBORAH LEVY
DEBORAH SMITH
DES LLOYD BEHARI
DEV KARAN AHUJA
DOUGLAS CANDANO
DR GEORGE HENSON
DR SAM NORTH
ED BROWNE
ED CUMMING
EDDIE REDMAYNE
EDWARD GRACE
ELEANOR CHANDLER

ELEY WILLIAMS
ELIAS FECHER
ELSPETH MITCHELL
EMILY BUTLER
EMILY LUTYENS
EMILY RUDGE
EMMA WARREN
ENRICO TASSI
EPILOGUE
EUAN MONAGHAN
EUGENIA LAPTEVA
EUROPA EDITIONS
EVA KELLENBERGER
FABER & FABER
FABER ACADEMY
FABER MEMBERS
FANNY SINGER
FATOS USTEK
FIONA GEILINGER
FIONA GRADY
FITZCARRALDO EDITIONS
FLORA CADZOW
FOLIO SOCIETY
FOUR CORNERS BOOKS
FRANCESCO PEDRAGLIO
GABRIEL VOGT
GALLAGHER LAWSON
GARY HABER
GEORGE HICKS
GEORGETTE TESTARD
GEORGIA GRIFFITHS
GEORGIA LANGLEY
GERMAN SIERRA
GHISLAIN DE RINCQUESEN
GILDA WILLIAMS
GILLIAN GRANT
GLENN BURTON
GRANTA BOOKS
HANNAH BARRY
HANNAH NAGLE
HANNAH WESTLAND
HANS ULRICH OBRIST
HARRIET HOROBIN-WORLEY
HARRY ECCLES-WILLIAMS
HARRY VAN DE BOSPOORT
HATTIE FOSTER
HAYLEY DIXON
HEADMASTER MAGAZINE
HELEN BARRELL
HELEN PYE
HELEN THORNE

HEMAN CHONG
HENRIETTTA SPIEGELBERG
HENRY HARDING
HENRY MARTIN
HENRY WRIGHT
HIKARI YOKOYAMA
HONEY LUARD
HORATIA HARROD
HOW TO ACADEMY
IAIN BROOME
IAN CHUNG
ICA
ISELIN SKOGLI
JACOB GARDNER
JACQUES STRAUSS
JADE FRENCH
JADE KOCH
JAMES BROOKES
JAMES KING
JAMES MEWIS
JAMES PUSEY
JAMES TURNBULL
JASPER ZAGAET
JAYA PRADHAN
JEANNE CONSTANS
JENNIFER CUSTER
JENNIFER HAMILTON-EMERY
JEREMY ADDISON
JEREMY DELLER
JEREMY MOULTON
JES FERNIE
JESSICA CRAIG
JESSICA SANTASCOY
JIAN WEI LIM
JO COLLEY
JOANNA WALSH
JOHN GORDON
JOHN LANGLEY
JOHN MURRAY
JOHN SCANLAN
JOHN SCHANCK
JOHN SIMNETT
JON DAY
JONATHAN CAPE
JONATHAN DUNCAN
JONATHAN WILLIAMS
JORDAN BASS
JORDAN HUMPHREYS
JORDAN RAZAVI
JORDI CARLES SUBIRA
JOSEPH DE LACEY

JOSEPH EDWARD
JOSEPHINE NEW
JOSHUA COHEN
JOSHUA DAVIS
JUDY BIRKBECK
JULIA CRABTREE
JULIA DINAN
JULIE PACHICO
JULIEN BÉZILLE
JURATE GACIONYTE
JUSTIN JAMES WALSH
KAJA MURAWSKA
KAMIYE FURUTA
KATE BRIGGS
KATE LOFTUS-O'BRIEN
KATE WILLS
KATHERINE LOCKTON
KATHERINE RUNDELL
KATHERINE TEMPLAR LEWIS
KATHRYN MARIS
KATHRYN SIEGEL
KEENAN MCCRACKEN
KIERAN CLANCY
KIERAN RID
KIRSTEEN HARDIE
KIT BUCHAN
KYLE PARKER
LAURA SNOAD
LAUREN ELKIN
LEAH SWAIN
LEE JORDAN
LEON DISCHE BECKER
LEWIS BUNGENER
LIA TEN BRINK
LIAM ROGERS
LILI HAMLYN
LILLIPUT PRESS
L'IMPOSSIBLE
LITERARY KITCHEN
LORENZ KLINGEBIEL
LOUISE GUINNESS
LOZANA ROSSENOVA
LUCIA PIETROIUSTI
LUCIE ELVEN
LUCY KUMARA MOORE
LUISA DE LANCASTRE
LUIZA SAUMA
MACK
MACLEHOSE PRESS
MAJDA GAMA
MALTE KOSIAN

MARIA DIMITROVA
MARIANNA SIMNETT
MARILOU TESTARD
MARIS KREIZMAN
MARK EL-KHATIB
MARK KROTOV
MARKUS ZETT
MARTA ARENAL LLORENTE
MARTIN CREED
MARTIN NICHOLAS
MATHILDE CABANAS
MATT GOLD
MATT HURCOMB
MATT MASTRICOVA
MATTHEW BALL
MATTHEW JOHNSTON
MATTHEW PONSFORD
MATTHEW RUDMAN
MAX FARRAR
MAX PORTER
MAX YOUNGMAN
MAXIME DARGAUD-FONS
MEGAN PIPER
MELISSA GOLDBERG
MELVILLE HOUSE
MICHAEL GREENWOLD
MICHAEL HOLTMANN
MICHAEL LEUE
MICHAEL SIGNORELLI
MICHAEL TROUGHTON
MICHELE SNYDER
MILES JOHNSON
MINIMONIOTAKU
MIRIAM GORDIS
MONICA OLIVEIRA
MONICA TIMMS
NAOMI CHANNA
NATHAN BRYANT
NATHAN FRANCIS
NED BEAUMAN
NEDA NEYNSKA
NEIL D.A. STEWART
NEW DIRECTIONS
NICK MULGREW
NICK SKIDMORE
NICK VOSS
NICKY BEAVEN
NICOLA SMYTH
NICOLAS CHAUVIN
NICOLE SIBELET
NILLY VON BAIBUS

FRIENDS OF THE WHITE REVIEW

OLEKSIY OSNACH
OLGA GROTOVA
OLI JACOBS
OLIVER BASCIANO
OLIVIA HEAL
OLIVIER RICHON
ONEWORLD
ORLANDO WHITFIELD
OSCAR GAYNOR
OWEN BOOTH
ØYSTEIN W ARBO
PADDY KELLY
PANGAEA SCULPTORS CENTRE
PATRICK GODDARD
PATRICK HAMM
PATRICK RAMBAUD
PATRICK STAFF
PAUL KEEGAN
PAUL TEASDALE
PEDRO
PEIRENE PRESS
PENGUIN BOOKS
PETER MURRAY
PHILIBERT DE DIVONNE
PHILIP JAMES MAUGHAN
PHILLIP KIM
PHOEBE STUBBS
PICADOR
PIERRE TESTARD
PIERS BARCLAY
PRIMORDIAL SEA
PUSHKIN PRESS
RACHEL ANDREWS
RACHEL GRACE
REBECCA SERVADIO
RENÁTE PRANCÁNE
RENATUS WU
RHYS TIMSON
RICHARD GLUCKMAN
RICHARD WENTWORTH
ROB SHARP
ROB SHERWOOD
ROBERT O'MEARA
ROBIN CAMERON
ROC SANDFORD
RORY O'KEEFFE
ROSALIND FURNESS
ROSANNA BOSCAWEN
ROSE BARCLAY
ROSIE CLARKE
RUBY COWLING

RUPERT CABBELL MANNERS
RUPERT MARTIN
RYAN CHAPMAN
RYAN EYERS
SADIE SMITH
SALLY BAILEY
SALLY MERCER
SALVAGE MAGAZINE
SAM BROWN
SAM GORDON
SAM MOSS
SAM SOLNICK
SAM THORNE
SAMUEL HUNT
SANAM GHARAGOZLOU
SARA BURNS
SARAH HARDIE
SARAH Y. VARNAM
SASKIA VOGEL
SCOTT ESPOSITO
SEAN HOOD
SEB EASTHAM
SELF PUBLISH, BE HAPPY
SERPENTINE GALLERY
SERPENT'S TAIL
SHARMAINE LOVEGROVE
SHOOTER LITERARY MAGAZINE
SIMON HARPER
SIMON WILLIAMS
SIMONE SCHRÖDER
SJOERD KRUIKEMEIER
SK THALE
SKENDER GHILAGA
SOPHIE CUNDALE
SOUMEYA ROBERTS
SOUTH LONDON GALLERY
SPIKE ISLAND
STEFANOS KOKOTOS
STEPHANIE TURNER
STEVE FLETCHER
SUSAN TOMASELLI
TAYLOR LE MELLE
TED MARTIN GREIJER
TELMO PRODUCCIONES
TERRIN WINKEL
THE ALARMIST
THE APPROACH
THE LETTER PRESS
THE REAL MATT WRIGHT
THEA HAWLIN
THEA URDAL

THEMISTOKLIS GIOKROUSSIS
THIBAULT CABANAS
THOMAS BUNSTEAD
THOMAS FRANCIS
THOMAS MOHR
THREE STAR BOOKS
TIM CURTAIN
TIMOTHY RENNIE
TITOUAN RUSSO
TOM GRACE
TOM JONES
TOM MCCARTHY
TROLLEY BOOKS
TZE-WEN CHAO
VALERIE BONNARDEL
VANESSA NICHOLAS
VERONIQUE TESTARD
VERSO BOOKS
VICTORIA MCGEE
VICTORIA MIRO
VIKTOR TIMOFEEV
VITA PEACOCK
WAYNE DALY
WEFUND.CO.UK
WHITE CUBE
WILL
WILL CHANCELLOR
WILL HEYWARD
WILL PALLEY
WILL SELF
WILLIAM ALDERWICK
WILLIAM CAIRNS
WILLOW GOLD
YASMINE SEALE
ZAYNAB DENA ZIARI
ZOE PILGER
ZOYA ROUS

Arkady by Patrick Langley
is published by Fitzcarraldo
Editions on 21 March 2018.

'Thick with smoky
atmosphere and beautifully
controlled – this is a vivid
and very fine debut.'
— Kevin Barry, author
of *City of Bohane*

Fitzcarraldo Editions

Contemporary
Sculpture
Fulmer

OPENING MAY 2018

THE HOME OF
CONTEMPORARY
SCULPTURE

Fulmer Common Road, Fulmer, Buckinghamshire, SL3 6JN
info@williambenington.co.uk

WILLIAM
BENINGTON
GALLERY

ZABLUDOWICZ COLLECTION
22 MARCH–8 JULY 2018

ERICKA BECKMAN
MARIANNA SIMNETT
BECKMAN
SIMNETT
BECKMAN
SIMNETT
BECKMAN
MARIANNA SIMNETT
ERICKA BECKMAN
MARIANNA SIMNETT
ERICKA BECKMAN
MARIANNA SIMNETT

FREE ENTRY
THURSDAY TO SUNDAY 12–6PM
176 PRINCE OF WALES ROAD
LONDON NW5 3PT
ZABLUDOWICZCOLLECTION.COM

Tŷ pawb

Is This Planet Earth?

02/04/2018 – 24/06/2018

Salvatore Arancio
Patrick Coyle
Halina Dominska
Dan Hays
Katherine Reekie
Helen Sear
Jason Singh
Alfie Strong
Seán Vicary

Curadur/Curator:
Angela Kingston

Artist preswyl/Artist in residence:
Tim Pugh

- Yr arddangosfa gyntaf yn Tŷ Pawb
  The first art exhibition in Tŷ Pawb
- Mynediad am ddim
  Free Admission
- Croeso i bawb
  All Welcome

typawb@wrexham.gov.uk
01978 292093

Llun/Image: Salvatore Arancio

Marchnadoedd —— Cymuned —— Celfyddydau
Markets ———— Community ———— Arts

Cyngor Celfyddydau Cymru
Arts Council of Wales

The National Lottery®
Y Loteri Genedlaethol

wrexham
wrecsam